DIRTY
South

Phillip Thomas Duck

DIRTY South

KIMANI
TRU
™

Recycling programs
for this product may
not exist in your area.

DIRTY SOUTH

ISBN-13: 978-0-373-83142-5

© 2009 Phillip Thomas Duck

www.KimaniTRU.com

Printed in U.S.A.

KENNEDY

Dedicated to Gilda Rogers of Frank Talk Art Bistro & Books and all of the wonderful teens from the Writer's Workshop:

Latisha Laing
Devin Velez
Shavon Shobe
Zhane Lane
Zakiyyah Godsey
Elijah Gisleson

Acknowledgments

First and foremost, I give honor and thanks to God. God, I thank You for my talent and blessings. I am eternally grateful that in Your infinite wisdom You saw fit to spare my daughter's life on December 9, 2008.

To my daughter, Ariana, every day with you is a complete joy. Thank you for your unbridled love.

To my mother, Melissa, thank you for your unwavering support and encouragement. To my brother, Michael, thank you, and as always, good things soon come. To the rest of my family and friends, thank you.

My agent, Sara Camilli, thanks.

My editor, Evette Porter, thank you. This process went much smoother than the first. (Smile).

Glenda Howard, thanks for the support and encouragement all of these years. I've enjoyed the ride.

My writer fam, keep pen to pad.

To all the book clubs, groups and readers, thank you for your support.

I know I missed someone. Charge it to my head and not my heart.

Come check me out in cyberspace.
www.myspace.com/phillwrite
phillwrite@aol.com

One,
Phillip Thomas Duck

"Now why's everybody so mad at the South for?
Change your style up, switch 2 southpaw"
Fat Joe, "Make It Rain"

chapter 1

Kenya

Tragedy.

Getting inside a black Land Rover with a virtual stranger. That is my tragic mistake.

Almost immediately I regret accepting this ride, and want out.

I reach in my purse, feel around, and realize a bad situation has just gotten worse.

"Can we turn around?" I ask. "I left my cell phone somewhere."

He looks over at me, smiles. His teeth are too perfect. Dentures, falsies, I guess. "Don't even sweat that phone, Kenya," he says.

My skin crawls at the sound of my name on his lips. He's creepy to the *n*th degree. I start to feel a tightness growing around my neck, cutting off my breathing. I'm close to hyperventilating. Anxious, nervous, scared. My heartbeat is a runaway locomotive. I try to calm myself. "We meeting up with Fiasco?" I ask.

Fiasco's my brother's friend, one of the hottest rappers in the game. Mr. Alonzo, the near stranger at the wheel of this black Land Rover, is part of Fiasco's security detail. Someone I could trust, I thought. Hopefully, I wasn't wrong. He freaks me out, but hopefully my mind is just playing tricks on me, and he's really quite harmless.

I'm about to get some time with Fiasco, that's what matters.

My brother Eric's been everyone's favorite nerd since he began the friendship with Fiasco.

I've been Public Enemy Number One, or at least it feels that way, with my popularity paling in comparison to my brother's.

Imagine that, Eric more popular than me.

Whatever.

Mr. Alonzo turns on the stereo. I'm not mad at that until a song comes on. Good music, just not for me. Mama's type of music. Marvin Gaye.

I wish Mama was here with me.

Someone.

Other than just me and him.

"We meeting up with Fiasco?" I repeat nervously. Maybe he didn't hear me the first time.

He ignores me, turns up the volume on the stereo.

"Mr. Alonzo?"

He doesn't answer, doesn't even look in my direction.

I'm beyond scared.

"Mr. Alonzo..." I wait a beat and then repeat his name. Over and over. "Mr. Alonzo...Mr. Alonzo...Mr. Alonzo..."

My breathing thickens. My pulse is scattershot.

Why won't he answer me?

I close my eyes, try to steady my heartbeat. The ride is smooth, like floating on a cloud. The music is crystal clear; Marvin's voice seems like it's coming from the backseat, no static whatsoever. The interior smells fresh, pine and something else I can't finger. But I don't want to be here.

I bite my lip.

Try to fight off the tears forming in my eyes.

Megan's Law. I think of that.

Megan Kanka, seven years old, raped and killed by a

child molester in New Jersey. The law was enacted in her memory—to protect innocent children. It made known sex offenders keep their names in a registry so the average citizen would know who lived in their neighborhoods.

A good law.

. But too late.

For Megan Kanka, that is.

Enacted after she was already gone.

My mouth goes dry.

The Green Mile, The Green Mile. That's all I can think of.

I want to think of that moment before I slid inside this black Land Rover. That split second before my bad judgment. Outside of my school, my brother Eric running for me and calling out my name.

Me turning and waving at him.

Then getting inside the Land Rover, feeling so special.

More special than Eric.

Riding off with Eric stuck at the curb. Stuck on stupid.

A little smile of victory on my face.

Eric was cool suddenly, only because of Fiasco.

I was always cool, on my own merit. Kenya, the girl the boys all wanted to date and the girls all wanted to be.

If I got in good with Fiasco, I couldn't be stopped. I'd be everything everybody wanted to be.

So I left Eric at the curb, slid in beside Mr. Alonzo.

I want to think about that split second before I got in the Land Rover. Change that decision.

But *The Green Mile, The Green Mile* is all my brain will really wrap itself around.

Mr. Alonzo is as big as Michael Clarke Duncan.

Nowhere near as gentle, though.

Not gentle at all, in fact. Evil is represented in all its forms on his face.

"Get out," he barks.

We've come to a stop.

I look out the window. It's completely dark out. We've

driven for I don't know how long. My mind has been on a continuous loop the entire ride. Don't know how far I am from home. When I'll be returning. Mama will be worried.

"Get out, Kenya." Mr. Alonzo's voice is covered in rust. *Needs WD-40,* I think.

"Do I have to?" I ask. A stupid question. He didn't bring me this far not to… Not to do whatever it is he wants to do.

He flashes a knowing smile. "I'm not gonna hurt you. It's gonna be fine. We'll have some fun, and then I'll get you home to your nerd brother."

Eric, standing on the curb, looking so sad as Mr. Alonzo drives away in a black Land Rover, a foolish girl in his passenger seat.

I'd give anything to touch Eric's hand now, hug his neck, tell him I do love him. I'm sorry for all of the hateful things I've said and done to him. He's corny, for sure. But he's my brother. And he loves me even when I don't deserve his love.

I'm sad.

Sad and lonely.

Sad and alone.

Except for Mr. Alonzo.

"I'm not playing, Kenya. Get out," his voice booms.

"This some kind of warehouse?" I ask, stalling.

"This is a playground, Kenya. This is a place for Daddy and his little girl to play." He laughs a horror-movie laugh. My stomach plummets as if I'm on a roller coaster.

"And what about Fiasco?" I ask.

The promise of hanging with the rapper appears now to have been no more than a handful of Skittles. Mr. Alonzo lured me into the Land Rover with that candy.

Mr. Alonzo shrugs. "Two's company, Kenya." He pauses, flashes that evil, dental-enhanced smile. "And three's a crowd."

No Fiasco.

Just Mr. Alonzo.

And me. Alone.

My tears start to flow.

Not like a river. No, like a wild, thrashing river.

Mr. Alonzo reaches over, wipes my eyes with his fat fingers, his thumb pressing a little too roughly against my eyelid. Not a gentle man by any means.

I hold my breath, sit rigid.

Mr. Alonzo brushes against me, grabs my door handle, pushes the door open.

Warm air.

Sticky and humid. Dark out.

I'd rather stay where I am.

"Last time, Kenya. Get your ass out. Now."

It's not that I'm being defiant. Not that I won't listen. I can't. My legs don't work. Won't work.

Pfff. The sound of Mr. Alonzo's growing frustration.

His rough hand is on my shoulder. Largest hand I've ever seen.

He pushes me out of the Land Rover.

I land clumsily, on my knee. Skin it.

For such a huge man, Mr. Alonzo is swift. He's out of the Land Rover and over on my side of the SUV before I take a breath to try and chase away the sting of my skinned knee. No more words spoken from him. Angry. All about action. He grabs my arm, rough hands digging into my armpits. Has me up on my feet. Drags me.

Just inside the warehouse, my legs come to life. His hand engulfs my arm still. But I walk with my own power for the first time. Legs are like water, but I walk.

Past a check-in counter.

Gun range. I've seen 'em on *CSI,* my homegirl Lark's favorite show.

Lark.

Wish I wasn't here alone. Wish I was kicking it with my girl.

We come to a stop.

Door marked Private.

"I don't want to go in there," I say.

Mr. Alonzo doesn't care. He shoves me inside. All pretense

is gone. He's no longer the big man with a faux smile on his face to try and set me at ease. The smile is gone. He's rough. Evil. That alone: evil.

The room is like an entertainer's dressing room. Everyone at school is big on my singing voice. Say I got Keyshia Cole beat by a country mile.

My mind is a mess.

Dressing room, yeah. I've made the big time.

A plush purple couch with a royal vibe is in one corner. A flat-screen plasma television in another corner. Large speakers hanging from the ceiling. Candlelight the only reprieve from pure darkness.

My dressing room.

But wait, Mr. Alonzo's face in the glow of the lights.

Like the Devil himself.

I'm not a star in my dressing room.

I'm a seventeen-year-old girl—about to be violated, my innocence stolen.

I close my eyes. Pray. Mama would be happy that in this desperate moment I prayed.

"You like the place, baby girl?"

I don't answer.

Mr. Alonzo's hand is on my wrist. I open my eyes and force a smile. I have to play along. Hope he has a change of heart, hope for something.

"It is beautiful," I say. "I didn't get to see much out there. Why don't you show me around?"

"Later. After we've had our fun in here, I'll show you the entire place. Now, why don't you get comfortable? Take off that hot dress."

Straight to the point.

I'm wearing a baby-doll dress the color of the North Carolina Tar Heels. Made of soft and sheer material. Not hot at all.

"I could use a drink," I say. "That would make me comfortable."

Mr. Alonzo doesn't answer, but I notice a punch bowl in the corner of the room. I move over there. Legs are still water.

I pause as I come to the bowl, horrified. The punch bowl is filled with condoms.

Behind me I hear Mr. Alonzo's booming horror-movie laugh. I close my eyes again.

Tears won't flow. I'm all dried up.

"Please," I whisper.

"Yeah, baby girl," Mr. Alonzo says. "Beg for it. I like that."

"Please, no" is all I can get out.

"Hmm, baby girl. Keep begging. Keep begging."

Mr. Alonzo's behind me, pressed up close, has me pinned in the corner. Smells like he bathed in Old Spice. His hot breath is on my neck. "Tell me how you want it," he says.

"I d-don't want it any way," I say in a stutter. It's difficult to get the words out.

He presses closer. "You're getting it, Kenya. And I'm giving it to you. Tell me how you want it."

"Alonzo."

Another voice.

Mr. Alonzo turns away from me, slowly.

I turn, too.

In the room with us now are Fiasco, my brother and some woman. Later, I'll find out her name is Mya. Sounds like the name of an angel to me, sent from Heaven.

Here to save me.

I smile. Only thing I can think to do. I smile at my brother.

"The whole family is here," Mr. Alonzo says. "Well, good."

Eric whispers something to Fiasco.

Fiasco nods.

Mr. Alonzo balls his hand in a fist, takes a step forward. A rope of vein pops up in his neck. He's the largest man I've ever seen. He steps forward with bad intentions.

Fiasco, my brother, Mya, they move forward, too.

It happens quickly.

My brother makes a fast move for Mr. Alonzo's legs.

At the same time, Fiasco makes a move for Mr. Alonzo's body.

Mya sends me some signal with her eyes.

Mr. Alonzo crouches low, like a baseball catcher, prepares for the two-on-one assault.

Mya sends me that signal with her eyes again.

Oh! I receive the message. Grab the punch bowl just a few feet away from me, turn it over, watch the condoms rain to the floor. Then I make haste toward the scuffle between Mr. Alonzo and Fiasco and my brother.

In one motion, I bring the punch bowl down on Mr. Alonzo's head. Eric rams his shoulder into Mr. Alonzo's knees. Fiasco heads Mr. Alonzo in the gut. Mr. Alonzo's catching wreck from every direction, from every angle. Knees, gut, head.

The big man staggers but doesn't go down.

I crack him in the head with the punch bowl a second time.

The bowl cracks, splinters. My second whack was much harder than the first.

I drop the ruined punch bowl like a hot potato.

So many punches are thrown. Fiasco, Eric, Mya.

Me.

Mr. Alonzo slumps finally.

We've quieted the beast.

Eric runs to me, breathing heavily. Tears are in his eyes. Mine, too.

We embrace.

Fiasco comes over, also breathing heavily. His eyes look haunted. "You okay?" he asks.

I sob as an answer.

Fiasco pulls me into an embrace, offers words of comfort.

"Watch out. He's back up," says the woman, Mya.

We all turn.

The beast isn't dead.

The beast is angry. Ready for some get back.

Mr. Alonzo moves toward us.

His shadow covers everything in the room.

Fiasco looks worn. My brother, too. They have no fight left, and neither do I.

I scream. And scream. And scream.

Music is playing. Not Marvin Gaye, either.

Mr. Alonzo fades away like an Etch A Sketch drawing.

India.Arie implores me to get it together.

I blink my eyes, try to focus. Try to steady my heartbeat. Try to understand my surroundings. Feels like I'm stuck in *The Matrix*.

I was having a nightmare. All too vivid. It's hard to believe I survived that horrible situation with Mr. Alonzo. The nightmare will not let go of me for a while. The only sway from the nightmare and what really happened with Mr. Alonzo in that room is he didn't get back up after we knocked him out.

Thank God.

"Bad dream?" I hear.

That's Donnell, my boyfriend, standing over me, concern painted on his face.

"Where am I?" I ask.

"My rest," he says.

I look around.

Donnell's room. Furniture is cherrywood and black. Blinds closed. Dark as a pit, how he likes it. No pictures on the walls. Donnell's not really into music, sports, movies or video games. None of the stuff the other boys worship. The CD playing is one of mine. Playing in the drive of his computer. He doesn't have a stereo. I don't think he owns even one CD.

I remember. "You were studying?"

He nods. He's taking summer courses at the local community college, getting a leg up on his freshman year of college. Donnell's practical like that. Practical and ambitious. The type of man women dream of marrying after they've wrecked their lives chasing after bad boys. Polar opposite of my last boyfriend, Ricky Williams, a bad boy to the *nth*. Nothing like Donnell Tucker.

Donnell has thin-legged blue jeans on, a burgundy T-shirt he wears tucked in, a black belt with a rock-star buckle, black slip-on shoes, diamond studs in his ears the only concession to popular fashion around our way. He's built like a running back but never carried a football for our high school team. His smile is one of my favorite things in the world.

"You were dreaming about...?" he asks.

I sigh. Shiver.

It's the tail end of summer. His central air isn't set too low. The shiver isn't about temperature, and Donnell is engaged enough to know that. His brows knit. "Thought you'd stopped having dreams about that."

I sit up on the side of his bed. "I had."

He sits down next to me. Arm up over my shoulder. "Want to talk about it?"

I shake my head.

He clears his throat. "This is a good studying CD. Calming."

I nod.

I don't have any words. So many thoughts running through my mind.

I had stopped dreaming about that near miss with Mr. Alonzo.

But my mind's been so troubled recently.

Ghosts are bound to rise when your mind is as troubled as mine is.

It makes me sad.

A lot of it has to do with Donnell.

The best thing that ever happened to me is Donnell's love.

And yet, it has me troubled.

Donnell smiles. "I was studying about these birds. They had me thinking about you, because they reminded me so much of you. And then you woke up."

He's the best boyfriend a girl could have. He's moved on, not dwelling on the dream, which is what I want. Of course, he knows that. That's why he did it. For me. That's the standard, ladies. A man that does the things you desire, *just because*.

"Birds? How I remind you of birds?"

Donnell is corny as Orville Redenbacher sometimes. I swear.

"Don't know." He pauses and shrugs. "They're called blue-footed *boobies*…and I just couldn't stop thinking of you for some reason."

I punch his shoulder. "Nasty."

"Girl, you know you like my style," he sings.

I hunch my eyes in surprise. "Been listening to the radio, have we?"

"I dabble," he admits through a thick smile.

I love Donnell.

Conversations with him are deep, meaningful. I'm on the verge of womanhood. He makes me feel like a woman. Reminds me of a part of myself I've yet to share with anyone.

My goodies.

I sit in silence. Think.

Donnell takes my hand after some time, squeezes it after every sentence.

"You've been happy." Squeeze. "Yourself again after that difficult experience." Squeeze. "Don't lose yourself again, YaYa. You're a survivor. Remember that." Squeeze, squeeze, squeeze.

YaYa.

Ricky used to call me Kay. At one time that meant something special to me. Now I'd rather a dude just treat me with respect, keep the games and lies out of our relationship. No pet name is required. But Donnell insisted on some kind of term of endearment the moment we became an official couple. Came up with YaYa. Sounds like something a baby does in its diaper. *Oh, look, Kenya did YaYa.* But whatever. Donnell treats me righteous, so I put up with it.

"I'm fine," I whisper.

He nods. Leaves it alone. Looks at me the way a man looks at a woman.

"So your parents gone for the entire weekend?" I ask.

"Yes, ma'am."

"North Carolina?"

"Vee-ay, Virginia. My mom's sister lives down there. My Aunt Regina. They eating catfish with their fingers right now, I bet. Drinking Riesling, but in paper cups, trying to cover up their *country*ness."

"Oh, yeah. That's what's up." I could care less about any of that. Have other things on my mind. I spider-walk my fingers up Donnell's arm.

Donnell looks in my eyes, deep.

"I have something for you," he says.

"Do you?"

Sexy, I'm feeling sexy.

"Yeah." He swallows.

"A gift?"

"You could say that."

I bite my lip, smile coyly. "Go ahead and give it to me," I whisper.

Donnell clears his throat. "Holeup…let me…let me get 'em."

"Don't keep me waiting too long," I say as he rises.

I watch him go. Watch his butt in his jeans. High and tight. High and tight.

He's back in a second, a large white shopping bag in hand.

"I know you're nervous about next week, so I got you a li'l something to hopefully set your mind at ease."

In a few days I'm off to Georgia for freshman orientation. A three-day event the school holds in August, a couple weeks before classes start for real. Preparation for the big change about to take place in the lives of incoming freshmen. I am nervous about leaving for school. Luckily, Lark, my best friend, is going to the same college. A pact we made years ago is coming to fruition. We'll be best friends for life, I'm sure.

Donnell's staying in Jersey so he can be close to his parents. Rutgers University. One of the best state colleges in the country. Donnell didn't feel comfortable putting miles between himself and his parents. They're getting older, he told me. I accepted that. Disappointed, because we'd be separated, but I accepted it. It shows Donnell's concern and sense of responsibility. That's why I love him so much.

Ricky didn't care about anybody but Ricky. Selfish to the *nth* degree.

Donnell hands me the bag. "A li'l something-something," he says.

I reach my hand inside, come out with a book. I flip it over, study the cover. It's a hardcover, sturdy. I've read this particular novel a thousand times, it seems. My paperback copy is falling to pieces. But this hardcover copy could probably make it through a million readings. "Toni Morrison's *Song of Solomon*. Thank you, baby."

"Open it."

I do.

Gasp at the cursive handwriting in black ink bleeding through the title page. "How did you...?"

"Last Saturday I didn't really have studying to do. I hope you'll forgive me for that little white lie." He smiles. "I drove out to Princeton. Ms. Morrison was giving a reading. Stood in line forever afterwards. Way too many women watching *Oprah*. Way too many. Homegirl's a rock star now."

I want to cry.

So many troubling thoughts in my head.

Donnell's being so sweet. Being so...him.

"There's more in the bag," he says.

I swallow that information and reach my hand in the bag again. "*I Am*. Chrisette Michele's CD. God, I love her."

"I know," Donnell says.

"I've been meaning to get this. Just haven't gotten around to it. Been so busy getting prepared for school."

"I know."

"Thanks" is all I can manage.

"There's more."

Lots, it turns out.

Smokin' Aces on DVD.

A case of Nature Valley's vanilla yogurt bars.

A dolphin key chain.

A twenty-five-dollar gift card to Barnes & Noble.

A poster of Taye Diggs. Another of Boris Kodjoe.

All of my favorite things.

My emotions are raw. So many troubling thoughts in my head.

"Get these posters signed like you did the book, and you'll be on to something," I whisper. "You know Taye and Boris are my future baby daddies."

"They won't live to pay you child support," Donnell says. "I'll take care of those pretty-boy Negroes in a second if they even think about going near my YaYa."

I'm his YaYa.

"You're making this so hard. So damn hard, Donnell."

"I'm going to miss you, too. And, yeah, it isn't ideal with you being all those miles away from me. But we can make it through this. I figure these three days you're away next week will be a good test run." He smiles. "Hope I don't fall apart, be outside howling at the moon late at night."

"So hard…"

Donnell embraces me, kisses my forehead. "We'll be fine."

I clear my throat. "There's something…I have something for you, too."

He smiles. "My baby got me a gift?"

I nod.

"Let me guess. Something for my car?"

I shake my head.

"You wouldn't get me a CD. Ditto for a video game." Realization comes to his face. "You bought me clothes? You won't quit until you have me in a throwback jersey and some timbs, will you?"

"Throwbacks are played. Where you been?"

"What then?"

I take his hand and draw the outline of a letter in his palm. "G?"

I nod, draw another letter.

"*O?*"

I continue on, five letters remaining.

"Another *O?*"

He's silent with the *D* and *I.*

"Goodies?" he says when I finish.

I nod.

"Been feeling some kind of way for a while. You don't pressure me, and I appreciate that more than you'll ever know." My voice softens as I go on. "I'm ready. I want to share my most precious gift with you, Donnell."

"Kenya…" He can't form any other words.

"You're so special to me. I want to show you my appreciation."

"You're… I mean… You're sure?"

"I'm positive."

So many troubling thoughts in my head.

He smiles. "'Cause we have time."

I pause. "No, we don't."

"What do you mean?" Smile remains.

I take his hand in mine, squeeze after each word. "Because after I give you my goodies, Donnell, honey, I'm breaking up with you."

His smile fades.

I'm not a know-it-all by any stretch of the imagination. That's not even cute. And if Kenya is anything, cute is high on the list. Right below ravishing and stunning. Coupla other adjectives I won't get into right now. I walk in a room and own it. Know-it-alls walk in a room and clear it out. See the major difference?

But there are certain things I do know for sure, and at the risk of sounding like a know-it-all I'm gonna go ahead and drop it like it's hotter than Boris Kodjoe.

Here goes.

Number One: Flavor Flav is not fine. It's the lure of television exposure that has all those women ready to bow down and kiss his crusty feet. I'm telling you. Even Flav has to know what time it is, without even peeking at that *ginormous* clock around his neck.

Moving on.

Number Two: Shakespeare and the Holy dudes that wrote the King James Version of the Bible had to have been cheating off of one another's papers. Reading either and actually comprehending the words you've read is harder than Britney Spears's noggin.

Doth says Kenya to ye.

Number Three: Text messaging needs its own twelve-step program. Thirty is the new twenty, and text messaging is the new crack. Definitely in need of a Textaholics Anonymous. Or at the very least an hour of dedicated intervention on Dr. Phil's show.

Dats da str8 truth, lol.

Sorry.

Anyhoo.

Number Four: I'm all that and then some. Yes, me. And I'm not being conceited or arrogant when I say that. It's a fact. Written in stone like Fred Flintstone's last will and testament. Undeniable, I tell you. Need proof? Check the vitals. I've got a body like Beyonce, a voice like Keyshia Cole, and I'm sexy as Alicia Keys. I'm R & B to the hilt. That's *rare* and *bodacious,* if you didn't know.

Lastly.

Number Five: Donnell loves me to death.

I think I might have messed up.

1 BABY…4 MEN TESTED…WHO'S THE FATHER?

That's the caption on my television screen.

I'm watching an episode of the *Maury* show. A bunch of stupid chicks that slept around and got pregnant. Now they're throwing darts at a board with the names of all the men they've slept with on it, trying desperately to figure out *who dey baby daddy is*. It seems like every day Maury has one of these paternity-test shows. I don't know what's worse: that Maury seems fixated on this type of show, or that there seems to be an endless supply of stupid chicks who've given up the goodies to any and everybody.

Oh well, better them than me.

Never say never. That's what Mama says.

I've always followed that advice, too.

I'm not so high-minded as to go on and on about what I'd never do, what situation I'd never find myself in. Never say never. There was a time I said I'd never date Donnell Tucker. Famous last words. Not only did I end up dating him. I fell in love.

So never say never.

But in this case, I can say with a certainty I'd never be in a position of not knowing who fathered my child. Never. Never. Never. There, I said it. Never. Never.

Oh hells no.

That's so damn tacky.

Maury prepares to open an envelope with Kaneisha's paternity results. It's her third time on the show, and this is the fifth dude she's had tested. But Kaneisha is absolutely positive this is Jamal's baby. A million percent positive, in fact. Jamal is just as positive it isn't his. He mentions how positive she was about Dante, and then Jared, and Trent and that lame Walter. "Can't believe you'd lay down with Walter," Jamal says. Kaneisha shoots back that she just messed around with those dudes, but she was really *holla*ing at Jamal. He was her main dude, for real. "Well," Jamal says, "why don't little Dante have my ears or nose, and why don't little Dante walk like me, either? You know I got that bop, Kaneisha. You know it be like music is playing when I walk. Like the new *Kanyeasy* is blasting and whatnot." Kaneisha agrees with a smile and a sigh. She has no answer for little Dante's ears, nose and walk. But she's still positive he's Jamal's son.

That's some straight-up buffoonery they're talking.

Little Dante is only seven months old.

Maury interrupts their back and forth, holds up the envelope again containing the paternity results.

My cell phone rings. It's Lark, my best friend.

Dayum!

I pick up. "Girl, you're messing up my *Maury*."

"*Maury?*" Lark says. "Forget *Maury*. We have to talk. I heard about you and Donnell. Ken, are you crazy? You're breaking up with Donnell. Are you crazy?"

"How do you know about that?"

"It ain't on TMZ.com," she says. "So I have to attribute my knowledge to my psychic intuitions. I'm touched, Ken. It's a lot to deal with. Be thankful you're not similarly inclined. A gift and a curse."

"Yeah, yeah. Who told you?"

Lark sighs. "Donnell mentioned it to Chuck Daniels. Chuck blabbed to Trent Greer. Trent's been trying to get some from Chante, so he's up in her ear damn near every day. He gave her the scoop. Chante gave me a call. So what is the deal, Ken? I can't believe you left me in the dark on this. Thought I was your girl. Talk to me."

"You are my girl. I was gonna call you. Let me finish this *Maury*, and we'll talk. I promise."

"Garbage, trash, degenerate nonsense…"

"What?"

"The stuff on *Maury,* that's what it is," Lark says. "Forget *Maury*. We need to be focused on you and Donnell. This is your life we're talking about here."

This I know.

And I'm not quite ready to deal with this latest dumb decision.

I'd nickname myself *BJ* if people weren't so gutter-minded.

Bad judgment.

I'm the queen of that.

"Lark, please. One minute, I promise. Just let me see what's up with this *Maury*."

"No, Ken. I wouldn't be your friend if I let this slide another second, much less a minute, so you can watch some dumb television show."

I snatch up my remote, stab the Power button. "Okay. Okay. What, Lark? What do you want from me?"

"How could you break up with Donnell, Ken? Are you crazy?"

"Why do you keep saying that?" I pause. "And what's those voices I hear? I know you didn't have me turn off my TV and you still got yours on, Lark."

"Don't be silly," Lark says.

"So what's that I hear?"

"We need to focus on the issue at hand, Ken. You and Donnell."

She's right.

I could use her counsel, truth be told.

"I should have spoken to you before I did anything," I say.

"Damn right, I'm your..."

Lark's voice trails off, and she gasps.

"Lark? Lark? Lark? Are you there?"

After a while, she answers. "I can't believe it, Ken."

"What? What happened? Are you okay?" My heart is throbbing in my throat.

Then I hear a small voice. Lark's.

"I'll be over in a bit, Ken. Can't talk right now. Betta we do this live, anyway."

"What happened? You sound upset."

"I am, Ken."

"What happened?"

"Kaneisha's a savage. The baby ain't Jamal's."

At that she clicks off, breaks our connection.

I'm outside on my steps when Lark walks up. I needed some fresh air to clear my head. I have to wonder about my decision. Maybe it wasn't the right one, as much as I thought it over before I talked to Donnell. He's absolutely the best dude I've ever encountered. Any girl lucky enough to have him down with her is blessed. I know all this.

But still…

Lark stops by the edge of the steps, puts her hands on her hips. "You got some 'splaining to do, Ken."

I remember the *Maury* situation. "So do you," I say. "Had me turn off my *Maury* and you were watching it yourself." I imitate her. "Garbage, trash, degenerate nonsense…"

She smiles sheepishly.

I don't say anything else. Hand her my cell phone. She furrows her brow, pauses and then takes it from me. She squints as she reads the text message on the screen. My homegirl needs glasses, but is too vain. And contacts are too much trouble.

I look off into the distance while she reads.

Lark reads the text out loud. "What's day without night? Good without bad? Left without right? Incomplete. Like me without you."

Despite my best efforts, my eyes start to water.

I keep my gaze off of Lark. Can't look at her.

"This is sad," she says. "I haven't been this hurt since Janet's wardrobe malfunction. You should be leaking eye water."

Eye water. That makes me smile despite my mood. Lark finally gave in to the charms of a dude. Donovan. Jamaican boy. Cute as all get-out. Smart and introspective. Just the kind of boy I always hoped for my homegirl. Life is good for her. It was for me, too.

Was.

"I see Donovan has you using his words," I manage.

"Say what?"

"Eye water."

Lark smiles, winds her hips seductively. "Pretty soon I'll be saying 'mash it up' if horny Donovan has his way."

That jars loose a thought. "I told Donnell he could have the goodies, but then I was breaking up with him."

"Say what?"

I look at her finally. "I was gonna give him my most precious gift...and then break up with him."

Lark waves her hand, shakes her head. "No Child Left Behind left me behind, Ken. I'm a little slow sometimes. I don't understand. Come again?"

Lark is actually very intelligent. Got skipped ahead two grades.

I clear my throat. "I love him, Lark. No doubt about it. But let's be realistic. I'm going away. He's staying here. Too much can happen. I learned that with Ricky."

"Donnell ain't Ricky."

"True dat."

"You need to bury that dead dog in a pet cemetery."

"Done deal. Trust me. I couldn't have moved on with Donnell if I hadn't. However, all good things eventually come to an end. But I didn't want to spend the rest of my life wondering what if. So I was going to make love to Donnell before I left."

"And then break up with him?"

The judgment in her voice makes me hesitate. "Well... yeah."

"That's some romantic shit."

I nod.

"My homegirl Merriam-Webster has a definition of romantic that you may not be familiar with, Ken." She pauses dramatically. "'Impractical in conception or plan.' Romantic."

I let that sink in. Then I drop my head. "I'm a natural-born fool, aren't I?"

"A little *ignent* sometimes, yeah."

"You're not helping."

"Keeping it one hundred with you, Ken."

"Donnell is wonderful in every way that matters."

"He is."

"Romantic." I sniff out a laugh. "In the more recognized sense of the word."

"My homegirl Merriam-Webster will allow you that."

"Attentive. Caring. Understanding. Respectful."

"You get no argument from me."

"I can't believe myself."

"How did he take it?"   .

"Badly," I admit.

He tried to reason with me. Couldn't. Drove me home in silence. Not a word when he dropped me at the curb. I stood in the street and watched him go. It was déjà vu for me. Same way it ended with Ricky. Kicked to the curb.

"He was inconsolable?" Lark asks.

I nod. "You could say that."

"Well, I'd hurry up and have another talk with him, Ken. If you're really having second thoughts."

"I wouldn't even know what to say at this point."

"Say something. Anything. Just talk to the boy. And do it fast. Have a sense of urgency."

"Why the rush?"

"You said he was inconsolable?"

"Yeah. Close enough."

"Chante also told me Melyssa Bryan was asking her questions about Donnell."

"That ho."

Lark nods. "Yeah, Ken. That ho might very well be looking to *console* Donnell."

I shake my head. "He wouldn't."

"Got yet another definition of romantic for you," Lark says.

"I'm listening."

"'Having no basis in fact.'"

"He wouldn't," I repeat.

Lark hammers her point home, too. "Romantic thought, Ken. Very romantic thought."

chapter 2

Eric

she looked like one of the girls in the Pussycat Dolls. Exotic and beautiful. It was hard for me to get my thoughts together. My brain didn't want to send the directive to my legs to move. *Nicole Scherzinger,* I kept thinking. Lead girl in the Dolls. Could it be?

I'd walked here. It took me about twenty minutes. Enough time to think about what I'd say to her. How I'd act. She pulled up, about five minutes after I'd arrived, in a silver Pontiac Grand Prix. That surprised me. I expected a black Range Rover. They say there are six million ways to die. I found one, then. Heartbreak. It was all over her face. The stride of her walk as she moved toward me. The way she shielded her eyes with sunglasses. The car she chose to drive.

"No Range?" I asked.

Mya shook her head and sneered. "It was nothing that I really needed, a material item. I gave it back to its owner."

Fiasco, her brother. He had a fleet of Land and Range Rovers.

"Gave it back, huh? And dropped down to this?" I pointed at the Grand Prix.

"Could've been worse," Mya said.

I frowned. "From a Range to a Grand Prix. How could it be worse?"

"Could've dropped to a Grand Am."

I eyed her. Nodded. She did have a point.

"I'm not calculus, so stop studying me so hard," Mya said after a moment.

Everything was calculated. I decided to remain focused on her lifestyle change.

"Sorry. Just wondering how I'm going to lay back and stretch my legs in this Grand Prix when I grow up to be tall, dark and handsome."

I was sixteen. Five-foot-eight.

Praying for a growth spurt.

Mya smiled for the first time. "You're a fool, baby boy."

"A fool in love." I embraced her. "Hi."

She pulled out of the embrace. "High is right. Standing there looking at me like that, looking like you smoked something today."

It was familiar and like old times between us. Like the first time we'd met.

We were at the Americana Diner. Prepared for a cozy lunch for two.

Mya reached in her purse. It was made of soft leather, felt like warm butter, and very expensive. I didn't know the label, but knew it was designer. So she hadn't given up everything, wasn't living like a nun in a nunnery. Mya's fingers came out of the purse with a green rectangular pack with white trim. Cigarettes. Newport. I hunched my eyes in surprise. "Since when do you smoke?"

She didn't answer, but greedily opened the pack, pulled out one cig, lit it with the flick of a Zippo lighter. She enjoyed two quick puffs with her eyes closed. Some color came back to her café-au-lait complexion.

Medicating herself with poison.

She opened her eyes, tossed a hesitant smile my way.

"Sorry. I've needed that for the past hour. Couldn't wait to stop for one."

I wouldn't judge.

"Hour. Why didn't you just smoke in the car?"

She frowned. "Not having my car smell like smoke. Uh-uh." She pinched her cig, took another pull on the cancer stick. "This is just a temporary situation," she said, squinting. "My smoking…a diversion."

"What are you diverting, Mya?"

I didn't expect an answer.

And didn't get one.

"Let's go on in, baby boy. I'm hungry enough to eat a horse."

"Betta finish all your food, too." I nodded at the Grand Prix. "Not enough room in your new whip for a doggy bag."

She pushed me by the shoulder. A beautiful woman, love-tapping me.

Confidence. Swagger.

I had it.

I wrapped my arm around her waist, walked like that to the door of the diner. Brushed up against her as I moved to open the door. Mya shied away from me. Something danced in her eyes. "You betta thank puberty for saving you, baby boy. I can't even get mad. You're a trip. Copping feels."

"I don't know what you're talking about, Mya."

She nodded. We went inside. Got seated immediately.

The waitress came just as quickly, took our orders. A burger with the biggest pickle wedge and creamiest coleslaw in New Jersey, plus a side order of shoestring French fries, for me. Chicken Caesar salad for Mya. Fruit punch and Diet Coke were our respective drinks.

"So what's good?" Mya asked.

"Everything."

"Junior year coming up?"

"Yup."

"Been shopping? You know you gotta be fly."

"Yeah." I smiled, looked her directly in the eyes. "Fiasco

got me a hookup with Kenneth Cole. You know he did their recent ad campaign? It ran in *Vibe, Essence,* I think. *Jet.*"

Mya slipped that jab, moved on to something else entirely. "You'll be driving soon, right?"

"Soon enough. Maybe Fiasco will give me the black Range Rover you gave back. What do you think?"

Our drinks arrived before Mya could reply. Didn't matter. She wouldn't've anyway. Fiasco wasn't someone she wanted to talk about. She blamed him for having that monster Alonzo around. Blamed Fiasco for what almost happened to my sister. I shuddered to think of how it would have ended for Kenya if Mya, Fiasco and I hadn't stormed in to save her from that predator. The three of us beat Alonzo's ass and then Fiasco calmly called the police. But he didn't have Alonzo arrested. Fiasco had a couple buddies on the force that did off-duty security for him from time to time. He called in a favor. He asked his buddies to escort Alonzo out of state, with a threat of worse if he ever returned. Get him out of Dirty Jersey. Fiasco felt that was the best course of action. Felt as if Alonzo would be hell-bent on revenge if he had to pull some time for what he almost did to Kenya, for what he'd already done to countless other young girls. Fiasco didn't want to have to look over his shoulder once Alonzo was released. And it would happen. That predator would get out. And it wouldn't be long. You didn't get a stretch for attempted rape. Sad, but true. I understood Fiasco's logic in letting Alonzo go. Kenya understood, too. She just wanted the ordeal behind her.

Mya was the lone holdout.

She'd wanted Alonzo in prison.

For what he'd attempted to do to Kenya.

For what he'd done to Mya when she was close to Kenya's age.

Alonzo, psycho that he was, wouldn't last long before he got himself in some trouble he couldn't get out of. He'd only managed to keep out of trouble before because he was under

Fiasco's close watch, working for his security detail. But things changed when Fiasco jettisoned him. Alonzo wasn't out of state but a minute before the law came down on him for some stupidity he got involved in with a bank and gun, I was told. He was his own worst enemy. Last I'd heard he was looking at ten to fifteen years, was sitting in a cell in Kentucky. His ass was bluegrass.

None of that mattered to Mya, though. She was still furious with Fiasco.

"Penny for your thoughts," Mya said.

I decided to just go ahead and roll the dice. Avoiding the major issue wouldn't make it go away. "Fiasco misses you. Misses his sister."

Mya sipped at her Diet Coke. Took some time with that. Then she calmly wiped her mouth with a napkin and spoke to me in a stern voice. "I'm close to losing my appetite, baby boy. If I do lose it, then I'll just leave without even finishing the meal. And we won't set up another date to break bread together ever again. And I can't promise I'll ever answer my cell phone if your number pops up on caller ID. Understand?"

I did. She didn't want to be pressed.

"So what's good with you?" I asked.

She studied me for a moment. Let her anger settle. Took another sip of Diet Coke. "Just finished doing some print ads. Shot a television commercial. It's all so boring. Mya the model," she sneered.

"Haven't done any music videos?"

"Eric..."

I raised my hand to signify peace. "I mean for anyone?"

Mya was the muse in all of her brother's past videos.

The beautiful woman who changed her looks for each one.

Was. Past tense. I hoped to change that. But I had to be careful how I proceeded.

Mya softened. "I haven't done any videos," she said.

Silence settled between us.

Mya eventually broke through the barrier.

"How's Kenya?" she asked.

"Getting ready to go off to college."

"Georgia, right?"

"Yeah."

"She gonna pledge? She gonna be a soror?"

"Couldn't tell you."

I had an idea. I wasn't sure it would work. But it was worth a try.

"She driving down?" Mya asked.

"Think so," I said. "I don't really know."

"You're pretty apathetic."

It was gonna work, I realized then.

I shrugged my shoulders. Part of my role.

"You're gonna miss her," Mya said.

I shrugged a second time.

"You'll miss her."

"I guess." I paused. "She's just my sister. No big deal. Siblings are replaceable. I'll just get a PlayStation 3 or something. And I'll be fine. Right?"

She slid off her sunglasses, folded them and carefully placed them in her pocketbook. Every move was graceful. She swept her head to the side, looked at me. Mya had beautiful eyes. Thick lashes that accentuated their beauty. I'd never seen her lively eyes turn cold.

Until then.

I held her gaze. My eyes weren't cold. They were friendly. I only wanted the best for her. For Fiasco. They were my friends. I loved them both. Equally.

She took a sip of her Diet Coke then set the glass down quietly. She looked at the glass for answers. Did that for a few seconds. I imagined at that moment she wished the Diet Coke was Grey Goose. I'd never seen her drink. And didn't know if she did. But then again, I'd never seen her smoke before, either. She was a troubled woman, with a hardened heart. Who knew how many devils she now worshipped?

"You spoke to him last, when?" Mya asked in a whisper

That surprised me. The frailty in her voice. That she was finally speaking about her brother.

"Yesterday," I said.

"He's where?"

"He told me he was headed to Charlotte."

She looked away. "He's doing okay?"

"Complained about them not showing enough love to a Jersey dude down in that part of the country. But other than that...said everything was cool. He sounded tired."

"Touring is taxing."

"I can imagine."

"All that travel will break you down. Wonder if he's..." Her voice trailed off.

"Taking his vitamins? Yeah, he is."

Mya looked at me, studied me, but kept quiet.

"He mentioned you always being on him to take his vitamins. Keep his strength up. Then he mentioned how much he missed you." I hesitated. "I hung up with him and texted you. Hoping you'd wanna hang out."

"Manipulative little bugger, aren't you?"

"It's all love. Trust me."

"Love."

That's all she said.

A chime rang out with each group of new patrons. It did, then. I looked up. Four girls entered. My age, huddled together like cheerleaders on a football sideline. I didn't pay them any real attention. Too concerned about Mya and Fiasco.

The girls were seated in a booth two over from us. Their chatter was the only sound in that area of the diner. Mya and I weren't talking.

One of the girls from the group got up almost as soon as they were seated. I glanced her way. She had a nice body. Couldn't see her face because she quickly had her back to me, was headed to the restroom. Puberty dictated that I had to get a look at her face when she returned. Like Mya had said, puberty was doing funny things to me, had a mind of its own.

Two of the waitstaff came from the back, ended by our table. "Burger?" asked one.

"That's me," I said.

The other placed the chicken Caesar salad in front of Mya. "Can we get you anything else?"

"We're fine," Mya said. "Thanks."

I started in on my burger right away. Mya bowed her head and silently said a prayer. That spurred me. I stopped eating and did the same. Mama would've been disappointed in me. We never ate a meal at home without giving God the proper thanks beforehand. I was slipping. That had to change. So much good had happened to me over the last year. I needed to remember how it used to be, and be thankful for how much my life had improved.

I said my quick prayer. "So much to be thankful for."

"Without question," Mya agreed.

"What are you thankful for, Mya?"

She looked at me. "That God has blessed me with a reasonable portion of health and strength."

"That's good. Anything else?"

"He granted me this new day. And not because I've been so faithful. But because He's so merciful."

"And forgiving. God is forgiving. We should be, too."

That made Mya frown.

Drop her gaze.

Study her hands.

Think.

Wasn't long before she looked up. "I guess I figured you'd want to talk about Fiasco. That you'd beat me over the head about my brother."

I nodded.

She continued. "And I came anyway. That says something, I believe. I might as well stop frontin'. I do miss my brother."

"Manipulative little bugger, aren't you?"

Mya smiled. "We love one another. My brother and I. In due time all wounds are healed, baby boy. Give us some time. You can rest. You don't have to play Mr. Fix-it anymore."

"Wanna see you guys right. Love y'all."

Mya nodded. "Ditto." Pause. "So do you...?"

Mya's voice became a whisper in my ear as I glanced up. The girl from two booths over was returning from the bathroom. Had to peep her face. I stopped chewing burger. My heart started to beat at a different rhythm and immediately sweat sprouted on me.

Everywhere.

On my forehead, my armpits, my hands.

"Baby boy, you okay?" asked Mya.

I managed to shake my head.

I wasn't.

Mya looked into my eyes, then turned to follow my gaze. The girl from the bathroom was maybe ten feet from her booth.

Mya turned back to me. Smiling. "I ain't mad at you. She's pretty."

"Pretty Young Thang," I said.

"You've got the thunderbolt, baby boy."

"What?"

"Ever watch *The Godfather?*"

"No."

"Good. You're too young. But anyway, the thunderbolt is when a man sees a woman and..."

"And?"

Mya laughed. "And he gets that dumb and dumber look on his face that you're sporting now."

"I feel ya. And it's even worse because I've thought about this particular girl every day for the longest."

"You know her?"

I nodded slowly.

Suncoast video store at the mall. She was more beautiful than anything I could ever put into words. And dressed to kill. True Religion jeans so tight they looked like they'd burst if she took a deep breath, a formfitting pink T-shirt, Steve Madden boots, a pink Yankees fitted cap on her head. She was Lisa Raye-brown, with hazel eyes and the body of a fully developed woman.

Endia Patton.

Same initials as mine.

I had a notepad at home with her name scribbled on it a million times. Scribbled a million times on top of that with her last name replaced as mine. Endia Posey. It had a nice ring to it, I thought.

"Tell me about her," Mya said.

I sighed, took a deep breath, tried to clear my head. "Met her the same day I met Fiasco."

A smile played at the corners of Mya's mouth. "The girl in the video store?"

I hunched my eyes in surprise. "Yeah. How did you know?"

Mya smiled. "Fiasco told me about that little episode. She handed you her cell phone, you typed your number in it, then closed it without saving the number. Fiasco said you were clueless that she wanted you to give her your number. You thought she just wanted you to check out her phone."

I groaned.

"I thought it was cute," Mya said.

"It wasn't. Believe me."

I'd struck up a conversation with Endia because I'd over-heard her asking a sales associate in the Suncoast store about a certain song. Endia knew the words but not the title or artist. I did know, though. Our conversation went well. I was the epitome of uncool then, but Endia was feeling me for some strange reason. But I did everything wrong. Fiasco had been in the wings, observing my game. Final verdict, I had no game. He came up to me after Endia left, wearing a bogus disguise, and schooled me from A to Z on what I'd done wrong with Endia. Thus began my friendship with one of the most gifted rappers alive. But I didn't get the girl.

That stung.

"You don't know how long I've been praying I'd run into her again," I told Mya.

"Well, now your prayers have been answered. So go handle your bidness."

My pulse quickened. All the dreams I'd had about Endia no longer mattered. The confidence I'd built up over the past few months left me. "What? Go talk to her?"

"Talk to her," Mya said. "Get her number. Call her. Fall in love. And after college, I repeat, after college, y'all make me some beautiful little nieces and nephews."

"I was kinda hoping to go half on a baby with *you*," I joked.

"Oh, were you now." Mya's eyes sparkled.

"With my looks and your intellect...imagine the possibilities."

Mya reached across the table, touched my hand, smiled. "Stop stalling. And go seal the deal with ol' girl."

I slid from the booth without further hesitation. Since meeting Fiasco and Mya, and becoming part of their lives, I'd grown in confidence. I had gained swagger. Seeing Endia sparked the memory of that time when I didn't have it. When I was uncool. Seeing her made me feel uncool again.

With a capital *U*.

But I would rely on muscle memory. I'd try and regain my swagger.

The girlish chatter in the neighboring booth stopped on a dime when I planted myself by their table's edge. My hands shook like I had Parkinson's. I put them in my pocket. Struck a cool pose. Or what I thought a cool pose looked like. I didn't know anymore. I was frazzled.

I looked Endia in the eyes. "Endia."

She blinked a few times. Frowned.

I smiled. "Don't tell me you don't remember me. That'd hurt my heart."

She blinked some more.

"Suncoast video at the mall. Last year."

Realization sparked light into her eyes. "You helped me find that song I was looking for. I don't even remember the song."

"You've got a good memory, baby girl."

Mya cleared her throat at our booth. Loudly. That got my attention.

Oops.

Baby girl was for Mya.

My bad.

"Glad you remembered me...li'l bit."

Mya coughed. Loudly.

I glanced over at her. She shook her head. A pained look on her face.

I settled my gaze back on Endia.

Ma?

Shawty?

Boo?

I was confused, unsure of which way to go. I settled on the simple. "Endia."

I heard Mya say "Yes."

Endia was looking at me like I had two heads. And both of them were the size of OJ's.

"So, how have you been, Endia?" I asked.

"Good. Getting ready for school."

"You 'bout to be a junior, too, correct?"

"Yeah." She smiled, and a funny thing happened.

My nerves calmed.

I could do this.

Muscle memory. Like riding a bike, you never forgot it. I had swagger. I wasn't uncool anymore.

I reached in my pocket, took out my LG enV phone. Slid it across the smooth table surface. Endia stopped it with her fingertips. "Let me get your math," I said. "I'd love to kick it with you sometime."

She didn't move.

"You don't already have a man, I hope. Don't wanna step on anyone's toes."

"Nah. I'm solo."

"Your math, then." I head-nodded at my phone. Confident. Direct. No wasn't a possible answer I'd accept.

"You're different," Endia said.

"You, too," I said, smiling. "You're actually even more beautiful than I remember."

One of the girls with her made a sound. A low whistle. I'd won over her girlfriends. I was in the mix like Robin Thicke.

"We had the same initials," Endia said. "I forgot your name, though."

"Forgot my name." I touched my heart, staggered back a step. Her girlfriends laughed. Endia smiled. "We still got the same initials. Think hard now. You're gonna hurt my heart if you don't remember."

It didn't take long. "Eric Posey," she said.

I smiled inside. Swagger was incredible. Swagger was a magic potion.

"I'll holla at you real soon, Endia. We can try and set something up for a weekend or something."

She still hadn't saved her number in my phone.

But my swagger was off the charts.

And I knew it wouldn't let me down.

Sure enough, Endia flipped the phone open and started to type in her info with the keyboard. She typed slowly, carefully. A smile on her face, biting her lip as her fingers moved. I imagine her stomach was doing flips.

I know mine was.

I finally looked at the other girls at the table. "How y'all ladies doing?"

They stuttered. Actually stuttered. "F-fine."

"That's what's up," I said.

Endia finished, closed my phone, held it against her chest for a moment as she eyed me. Then she finally slid the phone across the smooth table surface to me. I stopped it with my fingertips. Didn't take my eyes off of her.

"Thank you," I said sincerely.

Endia nodded.

"This is something seeing you like this, 'cause you been all on my brain," I said.

Thank you, Mr. Kanye West.

"You were nice," admitted Endia. "I've thought of you a couple times."

"Just a couple?"

She swallowed. "Maybe more."

I picked up my phone. "I'll get up."

I said that and moved back to my booth.

Mya jumped, startled. She'd been eavesdropping heavy.

"Nosy O'Donnell," I said.

"Whatever, Lionel Sissy."

"Who?"

"Nicole Richie's...forget it." She waved me off.

"Don't front on me," I said. "I handled mines. I went all in."

Mya smiled. "I'll give you that. I'm impressed. You were smooth."

I didn't reply. Listened to the whispered chatter from the girls' booth.

A lot of giggling was happening over there.

Smooth. Yes, indeed.

chapter 3

Kenya

Lark says, "Bare Escentuals. Ooh, Ken, we've gotta hit that up. Then I need some fish and chips from Arthur Treacher's."

I'm still reeling from the turbulence on our plane ride, and not the least bit interested in bath oils or body sprays. And forget about food. Especially fish. Oh hells no. That wouldn't be a good look with my stomach still doing flips.

"We don't have time for all that," I tell Lark. "We've gotta meet these girls."

Carolina and Tammy; they're our airport and campus escorts according to the letter the college sent us. In their sophomore year. Just last year they went through what Lark and I are about to go through. I'm looking forward to getting Carolina and Tammy's outlook on school life. The real deal. The raw uncut. The tell-it-how-it-is truth. What to expect, both the good and the bad. I don't want anything sugar-coated. I really want to know what I'm about to face.

I'm nervous. I can't front.

I think about the bag of gifts Donnell got for me. Just thinking about him makes me smile. I really do miss him.

Lark interrupts my thoughts of Donnell with a loud sigh. When I give her my full attention, Miss Diva pokes her lip out. "College is supposed to be fun, Ken. This is some stick-in-the mud mess."

"There'll be plenty of time for fun. The next few days are all about business. We need to be prepared for everything that is gonna happen this year. Or at least as much of it as we can predict. If we fail to prepare, we prepare to fail."

Usually, Lark is the voice of reason.

Today I'm the one sounding like a slogan on a bumper sticker.

Pseudo-motivational speaker on board.

"I know you're right," Lark says. "But I don't want to waste one minute, Ken. I want to let my hair down and have some fun. Fun, fun, fun."

I frown. "What's come over you?"

"What you mean?"

"You're acting...different."

"I'm out of the house. Out from under my mother's shadow."

"Honor thy mother and thy father," I say.

Lark studies me. Her eyes widen. She points an accusing finger at me, wags it, and something like a smile appears on her face. "I can't believe it. This is incredible. You're *scurred,* Kenya Posey."

I suck my teeth, wave her off, and then look away. I want to pick my nails, but I don't.

"Scurred," Lark repeats. "I can't believe it. Never thought I'd see the day."

"You're crazy. I don't know what you're talking about, Lark."

My drum of a heartbeat and sweaty palms know otherwise.

Lark grabs my shoulder, repositions me so she can look me directly in the face.

I hold the eye contact. I'm defiant. I refuse to back down. Refuse to acknowledge what is probably the truth.

Not willing to give Lark an inch of rope to hang me with.

"You're up here talking like Joel Osteen," Lark says. "What's that all about? Admit it. You're *scurred,* Ken."

"If you say I'm *scurred* one more time, I'm going to have a fit. I'm sick of that word. It's played and stupid."

"Scared. Petrified. Horrified. Terrified." She pauses. "I can go on. Aghast…"

"Okay," I whisper. "Maybe a little scared. You aren't?"

"Of course I am, Ken. But this can't be as bad as…" Her voice trails off into the ether. She has a strange look in her eyes I haven't seen ever before.

"You okay? What were you going to say? Bad as what?"

"Nothing, Ken." I don't press her.

We're in Concourse T at Hartsfield-Jackson Atlanta International Airport. A gang of folks moving around us, but not at the frenetic pace I'm used to seeing in New Jersey. That's why I chose a Southern university. Why Lark and I chose it. We both wanted a different pace, a slower pace, a more manageable pace. In Jersey it's hard to get your bearings sometimes. Everyone's in such a rush.

I'm as guilty of rushing as anyone I know.

I rushed to break up with Donnell.

A big mistake I've regretted every minute since I did it.

I wonder why he hasn't called, hasn't texted me, nothing.

The hurt in his eyes the last I saw of him stays with me. I messed up big-time.

Before I can start to feel sorry for myself I hear an unfamiliar voice. "Kenya? Lark?"

That breaks my reverie of Donnell.

I look in the direction of the voice.

Two girls that don't look much older than me.

One is thin, tall, toned but still feminine, has a short haircut, with a dark chocolate complexion set off with purplish lipstick. She's dressed in baby shorts and a tight T-shirt that shows off her track-star body. The other is short and thick, with long black tresses, as light as the other girl is dark, no makeup, but flawless skin, extra-light brown eyes that draw you in. She's wearing skintight jeans, and a T-shirt, as well. Both of 'em are beautiful. If they're who I think they are, then the stakes have definitely been raised. Wasn't but a handful of girls at school back home even close to as beautiful as these two. I was Queen Bee without much effort or competition. I won't be Queen Bee in Georgia as easily.

"Carolina?" I ask. "Tammy?"

Dark Chocolate smiles, offers her hand. "I'm Tammy. And you're which, Kenya or Lark?"

"Kenya," I tell her.

She repeats the same warm handshake with Lark.

Short and Thick does the same, introduces herself as Carolina and offers a warm handshake.

"Y'all are from New Jersey, right?" Carolina asks.

"Yep," I reply. "You?"

"Virginia."

I think of Donnell's family in Virginia.

It seems like everything leads me to some thought of my boyfriend.

Check that. Ex-boyfriend.

I shake that away and address Tammy. "And you? Where are you from?"

"Here, there, and everywhere," she says.

"Okaay." I'm not sure what that means.

Lark chimes in. "Here, there, and everywhere. Army brat, I bet."

Tammy nods. "You got it, Lark. Emphasis on *brat*." She laughs at that. "But it is what it is. I've spent time in North Carolina, Texas, parts of Florida, Maryland, even Kentucky."

"Must have been hard, moving around a lot," I say.

Tammy shakes her head. "Not really. I love a man in uniform. And there were plenty."

She's sassy.

Something I've always thought about myself. But I feel small and *sassy*less in comparison to her. I clear my throat, adjust my clothes. Suddenly I'm uncomfortable in my own skin. Of all my worries about going away to school, this feeling wasn't one I anticipated.

"There a lot of boys here?" Lark says.

Carolina clucks her tongue. "A few boys, yeah, but in some very good cases, men. Eligible brothers trying to get their learning on. You can't beat that. And good-looking, too. Shoot. It's a candy factory."

"Men," I mumble.

"Uh-oh," Carolina says. "Somebody's got men problems."

"She just broke up with her boyfriend," Lark offers.

I give my best female friend the evil eye. She feels the power of my glare, I suppose, because she looks away.

A smart move, because my evil eye can turn you to stone.

"No time for a broken heart here, Kenya," says Tammy. "Whatever happened in Jersey is done, homegirl. Brush that off your shoulders. It's live here."

Brush Donnell away?

Somehow I just can't.

Carolina sweeps her arm forward. "That's the Student Center. We call it the Peach Pit. I'm on the campus newspaper. The *Southern*. A lot of different school organizations meet up in there for business. I guess you could say it's the heart of the campus."

"That's all lovely," Tammy says. "But Beltran Hall is what you ladies need to be worried about."

"Beltran Hall?" I ask.

Carolina smiles. "Step shows. Most of the party stuff. Tammy lives to party. Getting her to open a book takes an act of Congress. Don't let her lead you astray."

Tammy scoffs. "Don't even go there, Car. I do remember a certain *lightskindeded* someone shaking her booty with a bevy of fine young gentlemen most of last year in Beltran Hall." She laughs. "And I said bevy. A nice journalistic word for you. Anyway, I won't mention any names. But this certain nameless female just happens to be our resident Lois Lane. And her name begins with a Carol and ends with a Lina."

Carolina gasps playfully. "Hater. I won't even tell Kenya and Lark how much you shook your track-hurdling booty up in Beltran Hall last year."

Tammy laughs. "I compete in the 100 and the 200. Get your facts straight, Greta Van Susteren. No hurdles."

Lark cuts in. "Forget facts. Just show me the way to Beltran Hall."

"Don't worry. You'll be seeing plenty of it tonight, Lark. Plenty."

"Tonight?"

Tammy sticks her chest out. "The Deltas do a little something-something to get you freshman ladies off to a good start." The twinkle in her eye shines like a diamond. I can only imagine what tonight's party is going to be like.

"You're a Delta?" I ask.

Tammy nods and looks over at Carolina.

Together, they break out in a chant.

A DELTA is
What an Ah-ka ain't
What a Zeta wants to be
What a Sigma can't
What an Alpha likes
And a Kappa luvs
and what a QUE PSI PHI can't get enough of…
OOO-OOP!!! OOO-OOP!!!!! OOOO-OOP OOO-OOP OOO-OOOP!!!!!!

Tammy and Carolina finish with a flourish. All smiles.

"That's what's up," Lark says.

Tammy high-fives Lark as Carolina looks on with pride.

"A party, huh?" I say.

Carolina touches my arm. "That's right. It will be pretty nice. You'll enjoy yourselves." She looks me in the eyes.

"And you'll find something to take your mind off that *situation* in New Jersey that has you with the long face."

"Maybe," I say.

"Ain't no maybes when the Deltas throw down," Tammy says. "Definitely."

It's nine.

The Delta event starts any minute.

And Carolina is freaking.

"Strep throat. This is sooo messed up. How could she get strep throat, Tammy? She's our lead."

Tammy shakes her head, sighs. "A three-woman song-and-dance troupe and only one of us can actually sing. Now that's trifling. We definitely weren't thinking."

"I knew we should have changed the dynamics of the group," cries Carolina. "This is a catastrophe. We won't be able to show our faces on campus after this debacle."

I can't help but think how happy Mama would be about my decision to come to school here, just by listening to Carolina speak. Mama's a sucker for articulate peeps.

"You and I can shake our rumps better than Katrina ever could, and I can hum my ass off," Tammy says. "Maybe the day isn't lost, Car."

"Hum your ass off." Carolina throws her hands up in the air.

She's the diva of the two, I've learned. She looks fierce in her crimson-and-cream outfit, though. And Tammy does, too. Maybe a hum-and-dance routine will work for them.

"We can't go on without a singer," Carolina says. "We're about to look ridiculous. I can't afford to look ridiculous. I have two more years to be concerned with. Oh, well, guess I'm transferring." She looks at Tammy. "Guess you'll be moving your 100 and 200 track-running booty somewhere else, too."

"Speak for yourself," Tammy says. "I'm incapable of looking ridiculous."

Carolina sneers. "That's right. You can hum really well."

"See what I'm saying," Tammy says.

Lark clears her throat. I have a bad feeling almost immediately. "I don't know if it matters, but Kenya can sing. In fact, she's very good. Best I've heard."

Carolina's and Tammy's heads snap around as if propelled by rocket force.

They look at me like Oprah has agreed to adopt them.

"Oh, boy," I say.

Carolina's on me, hand grabbing my shoulders in a death grip. "That true? No lie? Please resuscitate all of my hope. Please."

"With the proper warmup, and under the right mood, yeah...."

"I know this is somewhat impromptu, but could you give us a couple of lines?"

"Like what?"

"Anything," Tammy snaps. "Before my girl's blood pressure sends her to the E.R."

Her voice means business. I skip the warmup, jump right in.

I sing about being held like it was the last time.

Being touched like it was the last time.

Not wanting to forget the present is a gift.

An Alicia Keys ballad.

I end on a perfectly executed high note, and then stand quiet. Wait for their response.

Other than Lark's slight applause, quiet is queen.

Then Carolina breaks the silence. "I'm about to cry. I'm seriously about to ruin my dress. You've been sent from Heaven, I'm sure of it."

"Sent from Heaven," Tammy says. "That's Keyshia Cole."

"Sometimes life gives you lemons," Carolina says. "Sometimes it gives you joy, unspeakable joy."

I want to say, And *you* write for the campus paper? But I don't.

"You're gonna look great in crimson and cream, Kenya," says Tammy.

Carolina nods in agreement. "At least I have that heifer's dress. Just have to run out to my car and get it."

"Say what?" I manage to ask.

Tammy grabs my left arm, Carolina my right. They usher me off. "We've only got a few minutes before we perform," Carolina says. "We've got to get you up to speed quick."

I gulp, swallow. Look back over my shoulder. Lark shrugs, offers me a smile.

Friends.

The things they get you into.

Students are packed into Beltran Hall like sardines. Every year represented. I see doe-eyed freshmen and confident up-perclassmen. Crimson and cream streamers hang from the ceiling. Delta colors. A DJ, boxed in by two five-foot-tall speakers, spins the hottest records. Lights flash. Punch they swear isn't spiked fills several of the largest punch bowls I've ever seen. Females are dressed to impress, mucho cleavage, booties that make Kim Kardashian look anorexic. Dudes represent in grown and sexy attire, button-ups, slacks and footwear without a swoosh on the side. I don't think one of the dudes is less than six feet tall. Everybody's bunched up by the stage. I'm at the back of the auditorium. I scan the crowd for Lark. Can't find her. I silently cuss her out.

Carolina moves close to my right ear. "You're going to be fabulous. Speak it into existence."

"I'm going to be fabulous," I respond.

Tammy's in my left ear. "Don't mean to put pressure on you, Kenya, but it's all on you, homegirl. If we have to fall back on my humming, it ain't gonna be pretty."

"You can count on me," I say.

"The stage is your home," Carolina says. "You're comfortable and without fright on it. Speak it into existence."

"The stage is my home. I'm comfortable and without fright on it."

"Y'all ready for some more fiyah?"

That's the MC. A dude that's cuter than cute. Tall enough for the Lakers.

The crowd roars.

"Fuego," he says.

They roar some more.

Our music is cued. Carolina leads, then Tammy, me at the rear. We Destiny's Child-strut down an aisle carved down the center of the hall. As we reach the stage, shouts and screams fill the hall. I like the attention. My nerves disappear.

I move forward aggressively, grab the mic, shake my hips and swing my head.

And sing.

Better than I ever have before.

"'If I Were Your Girlfriend'."

Nicole Wray.

"What's your name?"

I look around, and then realize he's talking to me. It's the MC that warmed up the crowd, introduced Carolina, Tammy and me. *He* is about six-four. Dark chocolate, muscles for days, hair in waves. He looks like he belongs on the cover of a magazine. *Jet. Essence. Ebony.*

"Ebony," I find myself saying.

"Nice to meet you, Ebony," he says. "I enjoyed your singing. You've got a mean voice."

I shake away cobwebs. "I'm sorry, my name isn't Ebony. It's Kenya."

He narrows his eyes, studies me a bit and then smiles. He has dimples, perfect teeth. "Kenya...like the country?"

"Exactly."

He licks his lips. "I always did want to experience the motherland."

His voice is pure sex. "And your name?"

"JaMarcus."

"What year are you, JaMarcus?"

"Junior. You?"

"Freshman. Studying?"

"Premed."

Dr. JaMarcus.

Dayum.

I can just imagine opening up to him and saying *ahhh*.

"What are you thinking on, Kenya?" JaMarcus asks.

"What you mean?"

"You just got a look on your face. As if your favorite song just came on."

"Did I?"

"Yessir," he says in a singsong tone.

I don't have a reply. So I don't say anything.

"I'm wondering, so I might as well ask. You have a man, Kenya?"

The million dollar question.

I think on it for a bit.

Five seconds turns to ten turns to twenty.

"I don't know," I say at last. "I think so. Back home. It's complicated."

JaMarcus shakes his head thoughtfully. "You have a cell, Kenya?"

"Yeah."

"May I see it?" He holds out his hand.

Confident.

No doubt in his mind I'll give it to him.

I eye his muscles. He has running-back biceps. I bet he *did* play for his high school team. I hand my cell to him without any more thought. Watch as he types.

Same cell I haven't received any text messages or calls from Donnell on, I remind myself.

JaMarcus hands it back. "Saved my number in there. Hit me up sometime."

I gulp. "I'll see."

"Saved my number under the *N*'s. Not the *J*'s. Just so you know."

"The *N*'s?"

He smiles, dimples on display. All kinds of foolish thoughts run through my head. "Yeah. N for 'not complicated.' Unlike your situation with your n---- back home."

He turns and walks away.

Suave, smooth.

If this is how it's gonna be with the college boys, or men as Carolina says, I'm not sure I can make it through one semester without finding myself on the *Maury* show after all.

The conversation with Mr. Fuego makes me realize all the more why I broke up with Donnell. Temptation is fire, and I didn't want either one of us to get burned.

Last night's Delta party is a memory. Happily, it's a good one.

It's right back to business, which is fine with me.

We're crowded in the room the school provided for Lark and me.

A cozy li'l joint in the Tomlinson Building.

Tammy tosses a bottle of Dasani water my way. I bobble the toss, almost drop the bottle but somehow hold on. "Don't drink that, Kenya," she says. "Just hold it for now."

I roll the bottle over in my fingers. It is ice-cold to the touch, covered in a cool sweat. "And what am I holding this for?"

"It's hot out," she says.

I glance at Lark, send my best friend a telepathic message: *What's up with Tammy?* Lark shrugs. I try my luck with Carolina. There's nothing there, either. She doesn't even make eye contact with me, busy thumbing through a paperback novel I brought along for the flight from Jersey. *Only You,* a Francis Ray romance. I love happily ever after endings.

Back to Tammy.

"So," I say, "according to the itinerary the school sent us, you guys are gonna show us what buildings our classes are located in. Then there are some workshops later."

"No," Tammy says.

"There's been a change?"

"You're gonna be with me, Kenya."

"We're splitting up?"

Tammy doesn't answer. She starts stretching, warming up her quadriceps and hamstrings. Dressed in tight biker shorts, a green 7UP T-shirt and Reeboks with fluorescent laces, Tammy's in a no-nonsense mood today. Absent is the sassy homegirl with all the sharp remarks. I've only known her a short while, but long enough to miss her true self. Or, maybe this is her real self. If so, I prefer the other Tammy. This version is straight-up business. Not at all talkative. Introverted as opposed to extroverted. Stretching and whatnot. Like she's training for the Summer Olympics or something.

Whatever.

Do you.

As long as she understands I don't run unless I'm being chased.

I'll break it down for homegirl if it comes to that.

"Thought we were all sticking together," I say.

"We were." Tammy unscrews the cap on her own bottle of Dasani, takes a hard gulp, replaces the cap. She rolls her neck, stretches her arms overhead. She looks up, catches me eyeing her. "You ready to hit it, Kenya?"

Against my better judgment, I don't ask what exactly we're gonna be hitting.

But I do risk another glance at Lark. Get another shrug from my best friend. She's so helpful today. Carolina's still busy reading. She doesn't look up from the pages of the book.

"Aight, Kenya," Tammy says. "Let's hit it."

She doesn't give me a chance to question, to probe, to rebut. She's out the door.

I look at Lark, Carolina. "Well, later, I guess."

"I guess," Lark says.

Carolina's too caught up in the romance of Sierra Grayson and Blade Navarone to pay me any mind.

I leave those two. Head outside to catch up with Tammy. She's way up the walkway. Gliding like she's on skates.

I need rollerblades.

She makes a left turn. Passes two buildings, right turn, down a hill. I'm on her heels, breathing through my mouth and nose, trying to keep up. Finally, she comes to a stop. At a chain-link fence probably twenty feet high. Beyond the fence is a track with freshly painted lines for the running lanes. Several athletes are moving around, foreheads lined in concentration. A mixture of men and women. Lots of camaraderie from what I can gather. The smell of grass is heavy in the air. A crew of Latino maintenance workers is on mowers, tightening up the landscape around the entire perimeter of the track.

Tammy leans against the fence, does some more stretching.

I sidle up next to her, breathing heavily. "I'm not trying to be out here wheezing, Tammy. I'm sweating just from walking. I'm not down for a workout."

"I understand, Kenya. This is not for you. But I've gotta get some laps in."

"And I'm supposed to just sit around in this baking sun watching you?"

She smiles, the first I've seen from her all day. "Watching can be fun."

I narrow my eyes. "What's going on, Tammy?"

"What you mean?"

"Something's...not right. Something's been off all morning."

"Oh, oh." She nods thoughtfully. "Yeah, Kenya. I feel what you're saying. Sorry 'bout that in there. It couldn't be helped, though. I tried to just stay in my lane, you know? But it's tough. Carolina's in one of her funky moods."

"That's the pot calling the kettle black," my mama would say.

But I'm not my mama. "True dat." I pause. "What's up with her?"

And you?

"I love her to death. Carolina is the sister I never had." Tammy smiles again, raising her daily tally to two. She goes on. "All brothers. That probably explains why I'm such a tomboy. But like I said, I love Car. But she's by the book."

Tammy taps her lips, squints her eyes. "What word would she use? Think, think. She hates um…deviation. Carolina doesn't like to deviate from plans."

"And why exactly have we deviated?" I ask.

"Life ain't no fun if you keep it color-by-numbers, Kenya."

I put my hands on my hips. "So last night wasn't the end of our fun?"

Tammy smirks. "End of mine. Yes."

Why do I feel like I'm talking to Laurence Fishburne in *The Matrix?*

"Which means?" I ask.

"Which means, hopefully your fun has just begun, Kenya."

Deep voice, one I recognize.

I turn. Slowly.

JaMarcus.

Six-foot-four and covered in sweat.

In shorts and a wifebeater, his percentage of body fat must be in the single digits, judging by the lean muscles all over his body. He's like a statue, carved to perfection in stone by a careful, dedicated sculptor. He belongs in a museum somewhere. My legs turn to water. My mouth goes dry. My heart is running laps of its own. I wonder if he can see how affected I am by seeing him half-naked.

"Cool," he says. "That's love, Kenya. You brought my water."

"Tammy is good peoples. We mad cool. I'm the best on the men's side as far as track, and Tammy holds down the women's side. Matter of fact, she's probably better than I am. Olympics ain't just a dream for her. I can definitely see her representing in 2012. She trains like a beast. I'm trying to get that work ethic."

Modesty will get you far.

"Now, Carolina," he goes on. "She's a hater."

"So, let me get this right. You're the cause of all this… *deviation?*"

"Yeah, I guess. I asked Tammy if she'd swing by with you."

I suck my teeth. "I'm supposed to tour the buildings so I'll know where my classes are. Dang, JaMarcus. You've messed me up, boy."

I'm not really mad.

"I got you on that," he says. "Don't worry. I'll show you where everything is."

"All sweaty and icky…"

He hands me the bottle of Dasani. I think about his lips being on it just moments before. "I'm hitting the showers now," he says. "I won't be but a minute, I promise you. Meantime, you can peep Tammy out until I get back out here. Cool?"

"Yeah. I guess."

"That's what's up."

I settle into a spot in the bleachers.

Out on the track, Tammy is taking a turn better than my Acura.

She's fast.

The muscles in her legs don't take away from her beauty; they enhance it.

Five laps turns into ten, which turns into fifteen, then moves past twenty.

Damn! You go, girl!

She comes to a stop finally, breathing lightly, hands on her hips.

She pounds her chest, makes a peace sign, holds that gesture to the sky.

"Her mother passed last year."

I turn to JaMarcus. "What?"

He nods toward the track. "Tammy. Her mother passed last year."

"Damn. I didn't know that."

He nods. "Yeah, Kenya. She missed a little school, but got right back into it. Said that's what her mother would want. I have so much respect for her. She's my hero, for real."

"How come y'all never hooked up?"

What I really want to know is if they have.

"Not that I haven't tried," he says. "Tammy's focused. I ain't mad at her. She's helped me with my own focus." He sighs. "We're good as friends, though."

That honesty is surprising, real.

Mature, too.

This is the big leagues, a quantum leap from high school.

Am I ready?

"Gives you perspective," JaMarcus says.

"What does?"

"Tammy's mother dying like that. Life is short, Kenya. Gotta go for what you want the moment you realize you want it." His eyes find me. Something serious is brewing inside him.

Something's brewing inside me, too.

"Life is too short to waste on complicated situations," he says.

"Donnell," I say. "His name is Donnell."

Hope that mentioning his name will stop me in my tracks, prevent me from making another mistake I'll most likely regret. Hope is a good thing. A blessed thing.

"Donnell gets to kiss those lips. I envy him."

Fuego.

Fire.

I remember JaMarcus's words from last night.

Master of Ceremonies for the Delta party.

My lips are on fire.

They need to be doused.

"You want to kiss me?" I ask.

"Without question," he answers.

Life is short. Unpredictable.

Tammy's mother died unexpectedly.

College is a quantum leap from high school.

I'm ready.

"Let me settle my complications," I tell JaMarcus. "I'll be back in a couple of weeks."

JaMarcus, who will one day be a doctor, is ready as well. "I'll be here, Kenya," he says.

It's the next day, and we're back at Concourse T.

"It's been a real pleasure," Carolina says. "I'm looking forward to seeing you again in a couple weeks. You're gonna like it here. And you'll fit in nicely."

"That's so nice of you to say."

"JaMarcus is smitten." She smiles. "I can't say I blame him."

Everybody knows about JaMarcus. I don't know how I feel about that.

"And you sang beautifully the other night," she adds. "I can't thank you enough for that. You really saved us, Kenya."

"It was nothing," I say.

Tammy shakes her head in disagreement. "Don't be modest, homegirl. People are buzzing about us like never before. I hope you're gonna pledge Delta."

"A Delta is what an Ah-ka ain't," I sing. "What a Zeta wants to be. What a Sigma can't."

Tammy engulfs me in the biggest hug. "See you in a couple weeks, homegirl. We'll be waiting."

We'll be waiting.

I have a feeling JaMarcus is included in that number.

Carolina offers up a similarly heartfelt hug.

Funny, but my eyes mist over.

I've got two new sistergirlfriends. And one new…*something*.

"Just 'cause I can't sing a lick, does that mean I can't get any love?" asks Lark.

Tammy and Carolina laugh, give her a hug.

"I can hum my ass off if y'all need a fourth," Lark says.

"One hummer's fine, two's a crowd, homegirl," Tammy says.

Lark and I move off to board, to leave Georgia behind for the time being.

Back to New Jersey.

Georgia was nice. I had some great new experiences.

JaMarcus is heavy on my mind. But even more than him, I think of Donnell. Back to New Jersey.

And glad about it.

I have some complications that need settling.

"There I was giggling about the games
That I had played
with many hearts, and I'm not saying no names
Then the thought occurred, tear drops made my eyes burn
As I said to myself look what you've done to her"
LL Cool J, "I Need Love"

chapter 4

Kenya

I open my eyes.

My heartbeat is scattershot. Mouth is dry. The room feels like it's closing in on me. Another bad dream, the worst of nightmares. They're becoming a regular occurrence again.

I miss Donnell. He'd helped me through that difficult time. His love chased away everything that was bad in my life. We had a once-upon-a-time kind of love.

Until I rewrote the happily ever after ending.

I sit up on the side of my bed, stretch, focus my eyes, then reach for my cell phone on the nightstand. I check for missed calls, for text messages. No and no.

I dial a familiar number before I start to leak eye water.

She picks up on the third ring.

Her voice is cheery.

I can't handle cheery at the moment.

"What are you up to, girl?" I ask.

"Watching *CSI*. Why? What's up?"

"Nothing much."

"Everything all right, Ken? You sound funny."

"Yeah, I'm cool," I lie after a pause.

I hear the television background noise disappear from Lark's end. The squeak of her mattress springs. Soft footfalls across her carpeted room. A door closes. Mattress springs squeak again. "I turned off *CSI* for you, Ken," Lark says. "You betta come correct. Wassup?"

"Had another dream about Mr. Alonzo."

"Oh, Ken!"

"Been having them a lot lately."

"Well...is...was..." She doesn't know what to say.

I can understand that fully.

I don't, either.

"Well, let me go. Just needed someone to talk to," I say. The fact we haven't really talked is a small point.

"Ken? Holeup," Lark says.

"What?"

"Let's talk. You wanted to talk."

"Not much to say. I had another dream. Been having them again."

"Donnell really helped you through all of that."

I sigh. "Yes, he did."

"Stupid question. You haven't spoken to Donnell since we got back?"

"Been a minute since I spoke to him. He sent me that text I showed you before we left. And nothing since."

"Why don't you call him?"

"Best to leave that alone. Move on. Let him move on. I made my decision, gotta live with it." I pause. "Besides, I had a good time at school. We'll be leaving soon. Donnell is part of my past. A special part of my past, true enough, but still he's of the past. I don't want to close any other doors that might open for me."

Especially a six-foot-four door.

"Wasn't anybody down there even close to Donnell, Ken. Even JaMarcus with his fine self isn't Donnell. And you know that. Call your man."

"He's not my man anymore, Lark. I'm through with that situation. I'm sure he's forgotten about me by now."

"Just 'cause he went out with Melyssa Bryan doesn't mean he's forgotten about you. I bet it isn't even serious. And you should know. JaMarcus was all up on you, and you were feeling him, too. But at the end of the day you still love Donnell. Forget about Melyssa Bryan."

I feel light-headed all of a sudden.

The room is no longer closing in on me; now it is spinning.

I don't know which is worse.

"Melyssa Bryan?" I touch my stomach, consider hanging up, rushing to the bathroom. I feel nauseous. Mouth is salty beyond words. I'm about as close as you can come to vomiting. "Lark, I...I need to go. I'll...I'll talk with you later."

"Ken."

"I need to go." There are tears in my eyes, and in my voice, too.

"Oh my God!" Lark says. "Did I just put my foot in my mouth, Ken?"

I feel light-headed. Mouth is salty. The room is spinning. I'm gonna vomit.

"Melyssa Bryan..." My voice is barely a whisper.

"You didn't know. Oh my God! You didn't know. Did you?"

I lie down on my bed, put my free hand on my forehead. "No. I didn't."

Lark groans. "I've got foot-mouth disease, Ken. I'm so sorry."

"I'm cool." I say *cool* the way I spell it in text messages: *kewl*.

In another couple of weeks I'll be leaving for good. Starting a new life. With new people. New friends. New experiences. There will be plenty of new opportunities. Good dudes. College boys. College men. JaMarcus or somebody else.

That doesn't make me feel any better, though.

"Donnell is a good dude, Ken," Lark says. "And he cares about you a lot. That's not even debatable. He's not perfect. And neither are you. But you two are almost perfect *together*.

You're my best friend, Ken. I've never seen you as happy as you were with Donnell. Ever. Don't throw that away. I'm sure Melyssa Bryan doesn't mean anything to Donnell. But you should call him. Before it *is* too late."

Lark means well, but I'd consider her pep talk a soliloquy. Because I don't hear her, won't allow myself to hear her.

"Nope. Donnell made his choice."

"You kinda forced his hand, Ken."

That stings. Not what I'd expect from my best friend in this situation. But there's truth in Lark's words. And they say the truth hurts. It does. Hurts like a bad tooth. Hurts even worse sometimes.

"Okay, Lark, if you say so. I'll take the blame for what Donnell has done." I don't have the strength to argue. Don't have the strength to point fingers, assign blame. I'll just take it all. Own it as my fault.

"Not blaming you, Ken. Don't do that. Maybe I should have said something different. I'm sorry. But you have a choice. Do something, or do nothing. You gonna sit around feeling sorry for yourself? That's not like you."

"I'm fine, Lark. I'm cool."

Kewl.

"I have an idea," Lark says.

"Oh, Lord." I'm skeptical anytime Lark gets that edge in her voice.

Just a couple nights ago that edge had me on stage singing without any real preparation.

"I'm not kicking it with Donovan until later," she says. "If then."

"Okay? And?"

"You're not doing anything but sitting around feeling down, Ken."

"Thanks for pointing that out to me, Lark. I feel so much better now."

"I say we get *Get Smart* wid it."

"Which means?"

"Reconnaissance."

"Pretend I'm the President. Speak English to me…slowly."

"We can check on Donnell. See what he's up to."

"Oh, hells no."

I'd checked up on my last boyfriend. Ricky. Found out he had another girl pregnant. Came away from that situation feeling foolish, violated, used. Sometimes it was better to leave well enough alone. That's what Mama says. I'm riding with her on that one.

"Come on, Ken. Why not?"

"You've been watching too much *CSI*. I'll pass."

"What can it hurt?"

"He could be with Melyssa." My voice is getting raw. To match my emotions.

"And Michael Jackson could make a comeback. If *ifs* were fifths, we'd spend our lives drunk. Don't let *ifs* dictate your life for you, Ken."

I love my girl. Love everything about her. But I do get sick of her constant references to the Jackson family. Michael, Janet, Jermaine, blah, blah, blah.

"Lark…no."

"Come on, Ken. Go put four hundred dollars in the Acura…that should get you close to half a tank. And come get your girl."

"I don't want to know, Lark. Bad enough my mind is working overtime. Got all kinds of thoughts."

"That's 'bout as healthy as a yeast infection. And you wouldn't ignore that."

She's right.

I wouldn't.

I sigh.

"Something to be said for peace of mind, Ken," Lark says.

"You get on my nerves, Lark."

My give is like quicksand, a fast sink.

"Make sure you wear something dark, Ken. We want to see without being seen. Understand?"

Can't believe I'm gonna do this.

I try to soften the mood, chase away my fears, joke. "Want me to bring binoculars...duct tape, garbage bags, hammer and nails?"

"Don't be silly. What do we need with a hammer and nails? But bring the binoculars, duct tape and garbage bags."

Lark clicks off.

I can't help but smile.

I love my girl.

Acura TL. 2002. Close to a hundred and thirty thousand miles on it, and more than a few dents. But it's all mine. And I baby it like...well, like a baby. Unbeknownst to me, Mama had been tucking away a dollar here and five there since I was four years old. Around the time my father caught the fever and decided to cool off in the Bahamas, without us but with two Filipino sisters that used to live across the street from us. Nurses, both of 'em. And yes, I said two. Papa was a player to the nth degree. Anyway, apparently all those tucked-away dollars added up. So when I graduated in June, Mama entrusted that small bankroll to her boyfriend, Hollywood. He found the TL. Good work. The one useful thing he's done since coming into all of our lives. But I still don't like him. Grown man named Hollywood. Nuff said.

"This is gonna be so good," Lark says as she slides into my car. She's got a nonstop mouth. Has as many miles on her mouth as I have on my car.

"Hello to you, too," I say.

She waves me off. "We exchanged pleasantries on the phone, Ken. All *eight* times we spoke today."

"That many?"

"Yeah, girl. I've had to keep my eye on you. Feel like paparazzi trying to get pictures of Brangelina's twins. I was about to hide out in the bushes outside your house to keep an eye on you 24/7."

"There aren't any bushes outside my house."

"See how difficult this has been for me?"

I wince. "I've been that bad?"

"You haven't dangled any babies over a balcony, or driven with any babies in your lap." She stops, reroutes. "Why is there always a baby involved when a celebrity loses their natural mind?"

"Why are we always talking about celebrities?"

Lark shrugs. "I've been programmed and conditioned by the media. FOX network and *People* magazine have ruined me, girl. Totally messed up my impressionable mind."

All I can do is shake my head.

Buffoonery.

I grip the steering wheel, but don't take off. If Lark had her license I'd let her drive. My hands feel shaky, but look steady. My nerves *are* shaky, even if my hands aren't.

"Speak now or forever hold your peace," Lark says.

I wince again. "I'm a long way from a wedding. Can't even keep a boyfriend."

"Dramatic. Vivica Fox better watch her back."

Celebrities again. Maybe Lark has been ruined.

"Cut that," I say.

"Sanaa Lathan better sharpen her sword."

"Lark, focus."

"Jada Pinkett Smith better hurry up and get back in the game."

"I'm done talking to you, Lark."

She touches my shoulder, straightens her posture. "I drank at every vine. The last was like the first. I came upon no wine so wonderful as thirst."

I frown, look at her. "Okay, I'll bite, Lark. Who's that?"

"Edna St. Vincent Millay."

"Who dat? One of the stars on *Dancing with the Stars?*"

Am I the only person that doesn't know half of the so-called "stars" on that show?

"Silly ass," Lark says. "She's a poet."

"A poet? I don't know how you and my brother never hooked up, Lark."

Lark frowns. "Eric's like my baby brother. Please."

"You're both so damn articulate and well-read."

"You, too, Ken. Don't front. Reading Toni Morrison on the sly. And yet all you have listed in the Books section on your MySpace page is Zane and Relentless Aaron. That's false advertising, Ken."

"Anyway. So what does it mean? And how does it apply to my current situation?"

"What?"

"What you just said. Edna what's her face."

Lark waves me off again. "Ken, nothing. It just sounds pretty. And you've been down. Thought that might pick you up."

"That's not how it usually works, Lark. You don't quote poetry unless it has meaning to a situation."

"You don't usually break up with a boyfriend that is perfect for you, either." She shrugs. "Guess some rules are to be broken."

Touché. And ouch.

"Why do I feel like Laila Ali just punched me?"

Lark smiles. "Everyting gon be irie."

Jamaican slang. Everything is gonna be all right.

"Donovan," we say in unison.

And laugh like the girlfriends we are. For a brief moment, everything is all right. Everyting is irie.

No worries.

But that bottom will fall out shortly.

"I don't know about this."

"Don't get cold feet now, Ken."

"His car's in the front of the house. He's home. Let's just go." I move to put the Acura's transmission in Drive.

Lark grabs my hand, turns me facing her. "His car's running, sweetie."

"So?"

She taps the side of her head, makes a *duh* face. "Well, I'm going to use my intuitive powers, which have been sharpened by watching episodes of *CSI*, to deduce that Donnell is on the verge of leaving his house."

Just my luck we'd pull up and this is what we'd find. I wanted Donnell to be home, mourning me, not getting ready to go God knows where. I can't stand this. Another repeat of the disaster with my previous boyfriend. Ricky. You kick aside a rock and you're gonna find dirt and ants under it. I shouldn't have let Lark talk me into kicking aside this rock. My heart can't take it.

"Here he comes, Ken. Get ready."

Crap!

"He's dressed casual," Lark says. "Shorts and a button-up."

My heart thumps.

"Fresh haircut, too," she adds. "Got both diamond studs in and—" she squints as she leans forward "—is that a new watch?"

I glance up, nod. "New watch." Pause. "Fresh new K-Swiss, too."

"Could be going on a date," Lark says.

My heart thumps.

"I hate this," I say. "What happened to this all working out just fine?"

"If you find out it only took him a week to move on from you…that's working out fine, Ken. That's some good-to-know info."

Wonderful.

Knew I should have stayed home in my bed.

"Okay," Lark says. "Follow him. But don't crowd him. Stay a reasonable distance back."

CSI. Damn *CSI*.

"This is so exciting, Ken."

"A load of fun," I manage through gritted teeth.

We follow for a while before Donnell pulls up to a

7-Eleven. I park across the street in an abandoned lot, turn off my headlights. Donnell gets out of his car. Lark and I duck down but keep our eyes trained on him. His strut looks labored. Shoulders slumped.

The slump of his shoulders makes me wonder if he's mourning me after all.

Then I remember it started to fall apart between me and Ricky at a convenience store, too.

This has to be a bad omen.

"Wouldn't mind a Slurpee right about now," Lark says.

"You got me out here. Stay focused."

"What's wrong with black folks, Ken?"

"What'chu mean?"

She says, "I want a Slurpee. Craving one heavy. Trying to settle my mind on which flavor. And I keep thinking I have to go with red. But that's crazy, some straight-up ghetto-slash-black folks thinking. Red ain't no damn flavor."

"Buffoonery."

"Ain't it the truth."

Donnell exits the store, interrupting our nervous chatter. Lark taps me, nods at him. "Can't see what he has. Can you?"

"I bet one of those ninety-nine-cent cans of Arizona. Mango Madness."

"Damn, you're right." Donnell places the drink on the roof of his car, gets his keys together and fumbles with something. "You two know one another so well."

That's the worst part about starting over. You have to start over.

My stomach rumbles.

I deserve this, though. Wouldn't be here if I wasn't so foolish. If I hadn't rushed to break what wasn't broken.

"Damn," Lark says.

Damn is right.

In Donnell's other hand: a bouquet of roses.

"I'm sorry, Ken. I feel worse than—"

I cut her off. "You mention one of the Jacksons, and we're fighting."

"I'm sorry," she repeats.

I nod, bite my lip. "It is what it is." I start to laugh. "I'm sick of hearing people say that phrase. And here I go using it."

But it's true.

It is what it is.

Nothing I can do about the cards I'm dealt. But play 'em.

Donnell eases out of the 7-Eleven lot.

"You want to keep following, Ken?"

"Might as well see this through to the end."

I ease out behind him.

He turns off the main highway. Takes a lot of side streets. Residential areas. Comes to a bend in the road, bisected by a man-made lake, and turns left. Back on a less traveled highway. A Red Roof Inn and a Holiday Inn sign are illuminated off to our left up the road. Donnell turns into that complex. My stomach does flips. I hear Lark's heavy breathing beside me. Donnell passes the two inns. Follows the road out, turns left into a huge parking lot. A building before him.

"What's this place, Ken?"

I frown. "HealthSouth Rehabilitation Hospital, according to the sign."

Donnell slides into a spot up close to the building as I hang back. He appears to hesitate in his car, and then he gets out. Same loping steps. Shoulders slumped. He stops by the front of the building. The doors slide open. He steps away. They close. He pulls out his cell phone.

That's the play-by-play.

This feels like a play-off game in the NBA or something. Stakes are high. For me, at least.

"He's calling someone," Lark says.

I feel a vibration on my hip and look down. "Yeah. Me."

"Pick up. Pick up."

I do. "Hey," I whisper.

"Hey, yourself," says Donnell.

His voice sounds weary.

I've never heard him sound that way before.

"You don't sound well. Is everything okay?"

"Nope."

"Anything I can do?"

"You can park. Then you and Lark can come up with me to visit my moms."

"You spotted us?" Then I realized what he'd said. "Your moms?"

Donnell sighs. "Wasn't hard spotting you. You have that stuffed dolphin I won you hanging from your rearview mirror."

Seaside Heights. Boardwalk. We walked hand in hand that Saturday night he won the dolphin for me. The boardwalk was crowded. Donnell seemed so proud to hold my hand, let everyone know I was his girl. I felt the same way.

"I followed you," I confess. "I know it's wrong."

"You can tell me later why you've been following me," Donnell says. "I have to deal with my moms's situation right now."

"What happened to her?"

"Cerebrovascular accident," he says.

I hear the hurt in his voice. The disbelief.

I repeat that medical jargon, ask what it is.

He doesn't answer.

"A stroke," Lark says. "Who had a stroke, Ken?"

"I'm parking," I tell Donnell. "We'll be right there."

He says the saddest thing I've ever heard. Breaks my heart. Just one word. "Hurry."

chapter 5

Eric

1154 Sycamore Avenue.

That was the address of my friend Benny's house. Fool-ass white boy I just couldn't seem to shake loose. Through thick and thin, for better or worse, we somehow remained friends. We were like an old married couple. We'd fought, literally, actually threw punches at one another. We'd bickered verbally. We'd gone through cool-down periods where we didn't even speak for months at a clip. But in the end, we remained friends. Probably would be that way forever. It wasn't always easy, or comfortable, but I was glad just the same.

There were times when I seriously struggled with the friendship. Especially when I wasn't cool. When I was trying desperately to fit in. Posey the Poser and his white sidekick: that wasn't a good look. But after Fiasco came into my life, and the popularity that soon followed, what others thought didn't seem to matter as much. I became a leader, not a follower. I set the trends, established the new cool.

Damn near every cool black kid in my school would have a white friend they'd be ride or die with by the end of the year. Rainbow Coalitions popping up everywhere. I was Al Sharpton, Jesse Jackson, better still, Barack Obama. Changing the world from my little corner.

Yes, you can. My motto, too.

But 1154 Sycamore Avenue, Benny's address, still left a bitter taste in my mouth. I remembered standing in the doorway of Benny's grandmother's room just last year. She was a sick old lady. Fingers gnarled by arthritis, an unhealthy gray-yellow pallor to her skin. And the room smelled like six degrees of death. Her foot was on a banana peel, and she was toeing the line between this world and the afterlife. Dementia stole pockets of her day. But when she saw me standing in her doorway she seemed as lucid, as clearheaded, as she'd ever be.

She spoke on my mama.

Spoke about her in a way that would get most people slapped.

I was a punk at the time, not at all a fighter, but Mama was off-limits.

Regal dark skin, Vivica Fox frame, warm smile. Yeah, Mama was definitely off-limits for ridicule or disrespect. You didn't disrespect my *she*ro and get away with it.

But Benny's grandmother did. To my face.

Offered my mama a job caring for her because "wiping a white ass is a job for a Negro woman."

I was too shocked to respond, too weak to defend Mama's honor.

I'm still ashamed of my reaction that day.

I left 1154 Sycamore Avenue angry, slack-jawed, determined that I'd never return, adamant that my friendship with Benny had gone the way of the dinosaur.

Benny's grandmother died a few months later.

And as evil as she was, as set as I was that my friendship with Benny died at the period of his grandmother's hateful comment, I attended the funeral. Benny and I clasped hands after the service. "Thanks" was all he could manage. Nothing else was said. Nothing else needed to be.

I could have told him that my mama, she of the regal dark skin, Vivica Fox frame and warm smile, had pressed it upon me to attend the funeral, offer my condolences and support to a good friend. Even after I'd told her what happened with Benny's grandmother, the hateful words the old lady had uttered. I could have told Benny all of that. But I didn't. Mama made me promise I wouldn't make him feel any worse than he already did. I didn't break my promises to Mama.

I remember Mama's words.

"Some things you do because it seems right. Some things you do because you know God would have you to do them. You've reached your full potential when you know the difference."

And so I attended the funeral.

Even more surprising, I was back at 1154 Sycamore Avenue.

"Come, Eric. Gotta show you something."

That was Benny. The excitement in his voice was real; it had fingers. That meant that what he had to show me must have something to do with a video game. Benny was a one-track dude. When he watched television, it was all about G4, the gaming channel. His room was littered with magazines: *GamePro* and *EGM (Electronic Gaming Monthly)*.

So I wondered why he'd bypassed his winding staircase. Why we weren't climbing toward his room, the hub of the most extensive video-game collection in North America. No exaggeration.

I followed Benny down the foyer, toward the kitchen.

"What's up, Benny? You hungry or something? Grabbing a snack?"

I was worried he'd offer me some food. That would make me uncomfortable. I didn't eat in everyone's house. No disrespect, that's just the way Mama raised me.

He didn't answer. Didn't look back. Tiptoed. Of course, I tiptoed, too.

"Benny."

He looked back at me then. Quickly. Put a finger to his lips, demanded my silence. When he made it to the edge of the kitchen, he stopped, rubbed his hands together. Benny only had one interest besides video games that aroused this kind of excitement.

I came to his shoulder. "Who are you about to prank call?"

"Chill with that," Benny said. "I'm not about to crank call anyone. Get ya mind right."

Benny had gotten picked on and beaten up so much at school, it warped him. He changed how he talked, trying desperately not to be that sore thumb that stuck out. I didn't think I'd ever get used to him looking like Carrot Top and sounding like T.I.

"What's going on, Benny? Why are we whispering?"

"Will you chillax, Eric? I'm getting there. I'm getting there."

He pushed the swinging door to the kitchen forward just a crack. The smile on his face made his cheeks bulge. He looked like he had a mouthful of food.

"Peep this, E," Benny said.

I peered over his shoulder into the kitchen.

My immediate reaction was to wipe my mouth with the back of my hand. I'm sure I drooled.

There was a woman in Benny's kitchen that defied all laws of...everything. She was incredible. Eye candy of the highest order. And I immediately developed a sweet tooth.

She was wearing capri-style cargo pants and a wifebeater. She had the kind of body that would wipe your mind completely blank, make you stutter to come up with any coherent thought. Thick, strong legs. Tight, high-set butt. Pancake stomach, big, firm breasts. Her skin was the color of a Hershey's Kiss. Her black hair was braided in a thick knot and hung to her waist.

"I swear to God, everytime I peep her out I get hard as a Democratic Primary race," Benny said. "Sorry, Father."

Video game. Prank calls. And now sex.

Puberty had kicked in Benny's door waving a four-four.

Looking at the woman in the kitchen, I could understand fully.

"Dang, Benny. I don't know what to say."

"Ain't nothing to say, dawg. You just appreciate someone that fine and let her sexualize your mind. Sorry, Father."

"What's she cooking? Smells good."

"Carne gizado, canja, couscous, who knows. It will be good, though. She hasn't failed us once so far. Homegirl be putting her foot in it."

"What is she? Spanish?"

"Cape Verdean."

"Never heard of it."

"Me, either. Until she came. Then I had my head in Wikipedia like they had cheat codes to *Halo 3* posted on that mug."

I smiled. Looking at the woman in his kitchen, I could understand.

"It's a country off the west coast of Africa," Benny went on. "The Portuguese settled there back in the day. Brought over slaves from Senegal, Gambia, Guinea-Bissau. Her peeps were from Guinea-Bissau. Her mother was a performer. Her father dealt in textiles. They've both since passed. She has a brother still over there."

"You know a lot about her."

"I googled her."

"You found out all of that about her on Google?"

Benny shook his head. "Nah. I googled *her*. Asked her a million questions about her homeland, her upbringing. The equivalent of a Google search. I just say I googled her because…well, it sounds freaky. And I'm sixteen and horny." Benny laughed nervously. "Sorry, Father."

I nodded. "She's like…" I let it hang, couldn't come up with an apt description.

"I know. One day she was telling me about her native music—morna. And then her native dances—passada, funaná." He paused, licked his lips. "Coladeira. My goodness."

"Coladeira's hot?"

He grabbed my arm. "Dude, it's nuclear thermal."

I smiled. "Nuclear thermal? Not cool, Benny. Not cool at

all. What would the kids at school think if they heard that? A very unfortunate lapse in ghettospeak, my friend."

Benny waved me off. "I don't care. You see this woman, Eric. She makes you use words out of a dictionary. I'm inspired by her. If the kids at school don't like it, they can kiss my modular coupling."

I laughed. Benny didn't. He was caught up.

"What's her name?" I asked.

"Jule Gonsalves."

I repeated the name.

"She's fine as frog hair, E. The things I'd do to her if I did those things." Benny shook it off. "Sorry, Father."

"She'd have me praying, too," I said. "Girl like that lets you know how much you need Jesus."

Benny frowned. "Praying? What'chu talking 'bout?"

"Sorry, Father. You keep saying that."

Benny shook his head. "Not that father."

"Who then?"

"My father, E."

"Your father?" I knitted my brows. "I'm lost, Benny."

He pointed to the kitchen. "Miss Goodbody in there. She's my father's new girlfriend."

My mouth fell open. Benny's father had a black girlfriend. The opening in my mouth was large enough to fill with Benny's dead grandmother.

I left 1154 Sycamore Avenue with two clear directives from Benny: Call Endia, and see if she had a pretty friend willing to be Benny's date for a double. Jule, the brown-skinned Cape Verdean vixen, had my boy in an uproar.

Me, too.

My hormones jangled around like M&M's in a bag. I'd waited several days since seeing Endia, all to appear calmer and less affected than I was, but Benny was right. It was time to call her. I'd been waiting for that moment since she flipped my phone closed in the Americana Diner.

Old days, I'd have hesitated before dialing.

Old days.

But I'd reached the pinnacle of my confidence. No hesitation.

She picked up on the third ring.

"Hey, girl," I said right away.

"Eric?" I'd never felt a baby's bottom, but I doubted there was one softer than her voice.

"Yeah. What's good, Endia?"

I heard movement, like she was settling herself in bed. "Nada. Laying down. Reading."

"Sounds like my sister. What you reading?"

"Promise you won't laugh?"

"I'd never laugh at you, girl."

"Hmm. If you say so, Eric."

I loved how my name sounded on her lips. "E," I said.

"E?"

"Yeah. That's what everyone calls me. E. Or E.P. Know what I mean?"

"Mmm," she said.

"What was that for?"

"I don't know…E. You're different from when I first met you."

"True dat. That a problem?"

"Nah. Nah."

"So what you reading? Don't think I forgot."

She chuckled. That was a new sound for me. A development in the months since I'd met Fiasco. Prior to him, prior to me getting my swagger, it was full-blown laughter when it came to girls. Girls laughed at me, not with me, and they didn't chuckle. For the cool boys, but not me.

Oh, how things changed.

"If you laugh when I tell you, I'm not speaking to you again," Endia said.

I said, "Whatever. You just talking. You know you can't get enough of me."

I'd had enough conversations with females in the past six months that it was second nature. I was the teenaged version of Will Smith in *Hitch*. Smoove. With a *ve* not a *th*. Smoove.

"Well?" I asked when Endia wasn't forthcoming with the info.

"Ian Fleming."

"James Bond." I laughed.

"Eric," she screamed.

"Said call me E," I chided in my stern voice.

"My bad," Endia said. "You laughed at me, though, E. I'm mad at you."

Mad, but she hadn't hung up. My hypothesis tested correct. Swagger was a magic potion, for sure.

"I didn't mean to laugh, Endia. Nothing wrong with James Bond. Just wasn't what I expected. Pretty Young Thang like you. I was expecting Cheetah Girls, for sure."

"No." I could sense a frown over the fiber optics. "I don't know. James Bond is so…so…cool. Fleming's British, and I don't understand a lot of the language in the books, but…" She caught herself. "This is silly."

"You picture yourself with a dude like Bond. Suave. Debonair. Tough. Intelligent." I paused. "Cool."

"Yeah," she admitted.

I cleared my throat. "Today's your lucky day, Endia. It just so happens I'm all of those things."

"I know it," she said, and a smile broke across my face that I can't even describe.

"So what happened?"

Benny, my compadre.

"We talked," I said.

"And?"

"She's cool, Benny. I like her even more after talking to her. She's smart. Funny."

"Sociable?" Benny wanted to know. "Has a strong social network?"

"Yeah, I guess. She's got over two hundred friends on MySpace."

"And I surmise some of them are females?"

Surmise?

It was funny how the real Benny surfaced when he was on edge. He wanted to know if I got him the hookup with one of Endia's girlfriends. Unfortunately for him, I was in a playful mood. I wasn't about to give up the goods that early in the conversation. Wanted to see him sweat.

"Yeah, I guess you could *surmise* that," I said. "In fact, I believe she has a lot of girlfriends. She sounds like a popular girl. She mentioned quite a few friends, in fact."

"Anybody interesting?"

"Dude James sounded like a for-real brother. She's known him since they were little. He wants to write plays. Their school did one of his productions last year. She said the response was great."

"So he's a homosexual?" Benny scoffed.

"Not at all," I said. "Endia says he's got game."

"So his boyfriend's the homosexual?"

I briefly moved the phone from my mouth and laughed. "Stereotyping. You of all people should know better, Benny."

"Call it how I see it. What else? She mention any other friends?"

"Dude named Charles."

"What he do? Hair and makeup for the cast in James's play?"

I moved the phone away and laughed again. Benny was really on edge.

"Charles is quarterback on the football team."

"You sure it ain't field hockey?" Benny sighed in frustration. "This girl have any straight female friends, E?"

"Well, I told you she was with a bunch of girls when I saw her at the diner."

"Yes. You did. So what's up?"

His voice was sharp enough to cut glass. Thick glass.

I couldn't help myself.

I laughed long and hard. And I didn't move the phone away.

"Eric, Eric...yo, E." Benny's attempts to get my attention just made my fit of laughter worse.

But he held on until I calmed myself.

"I'm sorry, Benny," I said. "I'm just messing with you."

"Yeah, mess with Benny. Pick on Benny. Have fun at the white boy's expense. Tease and humiliate good ole Benny—"

I cut into his rant. "Tanya."

As dramatic as he was being, he stopped immediately. "That's my shawty, E?"

"You came down off your woe-is-me platform awful quick."

Benny snickered. "I was just feeding into your black guilt for the way your people have mistreated nerdish white boys down through the centuries."

We'd come a long way. Not too long ago we couldn't joke about race.

"Well, hopefully Tanya will make up for the mistreatment. Endia said she's pretty."

Benny whooped and hollered on his end, actually dropped the phone. Sounded like he kicked it around on the ground some, too.

I held on.

When he came back to the phone, he was out of breath. "Sorry about that, dawg. It's all good."

I hung up on him. He rang back before I blinked an eye.

chapter 6

Lark

what was that smell?

A million smells mingled as one. The No. 56 special, shrimp fried rice, from Sultan's, the Chinese spot on the corner, stale urine and body stench from the homeless vacationers lounging in their cardboard condos behind the building, sweat and tes-tosterone from the li'l gangbangers who cruised the block in cars with deep-tinted windows and earth-shattering sound systems. The scent of poverty, depression.

What was that sound?

Cars screaming out in pain, violated, their stereos ripped from their guts. Old school Mahalia Jackson hymns coming from Hope Eternal, the fire-and-brimstone church next to Sultan's. Moans from the johns down in the alley spending money their wives weren't aware of for a quick pleasure their wives would never know about, either. Gunshots, poverty, depression.

In apartment 309, the smell was buttered toast and Jimmy Dean sausage patties, cut peaches in a bowl, fresh orange juice. That sound was the television, turned up too loud, an episode of *CSI*, the third of ten shows in an all-day marathon.

"Don't know why you always watching this mess. It's a waste of time. All that big word mumbo jumbo you don't even understand."

"I do understand it," Lark told her mother. "I've watched enough, and I've caught on. And sometimes, with big words, if you listen to the next thing they say, that'll give you a clue what the big word meant. That's known as learning through context."

Lark's mother stopped midstride, settled in that real estate in the center of the kitchen, hands on her ample hips, flowery housedress hanging off her thick and overworked frame, run-down slippers on her bad feet, her hair in curlers. "Right," she said. "Thanks for that helpful tip. Learning through context. I have to remember that. Maybe it'll help me with the laundry, or at the grocery store, or when I'm cleaning the bathroom."

Lark hated her mother's sarcasm. But she wasn't in the mood for a fight. "I'm sorry, Mama. I wasn't trying to insult you."

"No need to apologize. It was a very helpful tip. I'd almost forgotten you were so intelligent."

Still sarcastic, and she said intelligent as if it were four words, emphasizing each syllable. It was an indictment the way she said it. Lark was guilty of something. Lark dropped her head, looked down at her plate of food, avoided her mother's gaze. Guilty.

As charged.

Lark's mother's name was Carmen Edwards, but everyone called her Honey.

'Cause she was beautiful and brown-skinned and her walk made men lick their lips…and fingers.

At least that's how it was back in the day. Today she was burned-out. Used up.

Honey. Somehow the name endured.

"I'm turning this mess off," Honey said. "Can't stand another fingerprint analysis. Another DNA blueprint. One more forensic discovery and I'ma have a headache."

Fingerprint analysis.

DNA blueprint.

Forensic discovery.

She said those words with the same disdain as she'd used for *intelligence,* a while before. With the same rough manner that she'd accosted Jin with for trying to sell her rotten peaches down at the Farmer's Market. Honey was a rough woman, no question about it. Everything, or at the very least, most things, with her were handled roughly.

"Go ahead and turn it, Mama," Lark said. "I've seen enough, too."

Lark hadn't really. She was curious about how it would all end. But whatever.

"I am turning it. Don't need your permission. You my chile."

Even when Lark surrendered quietly, which was often, it was still a fight. Her mother liked anarchy. Chaos. Her swollen lip was the latest evidence. Lark's father didn't like anarchy. Chaos. It made him mad. Made him loose with his fists.

"And I'm not putting on any of them judge shows, either," Honey said. "I don't give a shit who's liable for what. What the plaintiff has got to say. Or what is a suitable resolution to any landlord/tenant dispute. I'm watching my soaps. You hear?"

"That's fine, Mama."

"It's gonna have to be fine."

"It sure is."

"You sassing me, girl?"

"No, Mama. Not at all."

"I brought you in this world. I'll take you out of it, too."

"Would you please?" Lark whispered.

But apparently not quietly enough.

Honey was on her in a split second. Shaking Lark. Slapping her, too. "Shake some sense into you, girl," Honey muttered as she finished her onslaught.

Lark brushed her wrinkled clothes, clenched her jaws. Eyes wide, unblinking, daring any tears to form. It was a familiar scene, not nearly as surprising as the first time her mother had roughed her up. But whatever. It was what it was. She did what she had to in order to coexist with her parental units. Parental units. Kenya thought that just another of Lark's creative ways of saying something differently than anyone else. Part of Lark's uniqueness. But it was born out of necessity. Lark couldn't bear to call them parents. Couldn't. Wouldn't.

Honey backed away, breathing heavily. A look in her eyes that screamed for a rabies shot.

"Feel better, now?" Lark ventured. "Purged?"

Sassing for real.

But so what?

What did she have to lose?

"That mouth of yours gonna get you in a world of hurt," Honey said.

Lark calmed herself. Regardless of the situation, respect was due her mother. "I'm sorry, Mama. I was out of line."

"Sorry's right. Be glad when you get on up out of here."

"Couple of weeks," Lark said.

"Fall flat on your face," Honey replied with a sneer. "College. Don't know how you got it in your fool head you were built for somebody's college."

Lark couldn't see herself walking down some dusty road in Baghdad.

She couldn't see herself folding clothes, building displays at Macy's.

She wasn't looking to be some man's slave...er, wife.

So college.

Worked damn hard. Skipped ahead two grades.

The quicker out of her house, the better.

"Paying all of this money for college," said Honey.

Scholarships footed ninety percent of the bill. Lark was gonna work off the rest.

But she wasn't about to point any of this out to her mother.

"And I appreciate it, Mama," she said. "All of your sacrifice."

Honey's eyes tightened. "Keep it up, girl. That smart mouth. Keep it up."

It was a hopeless situation.

Like Michael Jackson selling *Thriller*-type numbers again.

Lark smiled.

Kenya always said Lark was obsessed with the Jacksons. It was true, she had to admit.

"Wipe that smile off your face, girl. This ain't Dave Chapelle. We're talking about some serious issues."

Were they?

Okay. Lark did as told. Wiped the smile off her face.

"I tell you, girl," Honey said, "things sure is gonna change around here with you gone. I'm so looking forward to it."

"I'm sure you and daddy will have to *fight* each other off," Lark said. "Maybe I'll get that little sister I always wanted." She immediately bit into her Jimmy Dean sausage patty. Closed her eyes and savored the flavor. The little things.

"And your fast tail better not take up with some boy and have to come slinking home before the end of the first semester like I—" Honey stopped abruptly. As if she'd been hit cleanly by a stray from the gangbangers outside her window.

Lark wasn't a fast tail. But she was fast. Mentally. Little escaped her.

"Wait a minute," she said. "You were in college when you got pregnant with me, Mama?"

Honey waved her off. "I'm done talking about this nonsense."

Lark let it go.

Honey took a rag and wiped down the counter.

Her swollen lip throbbed, head ached.

Rider University.

Class of '96.

If only.

If only.

* * *

World's most colorful fighter.

Cassius Clay, later Muhammad Ali, had those words painted on the side of his travel bus. Fiasco had read about it in David Remnick's book *King of the World,* a piece set around Ali's dramatic fights with Sonny Liston.

World's most colorful MC.

Not rapper. MC. Master of Ceremonies.

World's most colorful MC.

Fiasco had the words airbrushed on the side of his own travel bus.

He was traveling on the bus. Headed for a little club in North Carolina. He was reclined on a pull-down bed. Long, Jordan-sized shorts on, a wifebeater, white socks. Book in hand. Reading *King of the World.* Again. About the twentieth time. Sparked because Remnick, the author, also editor of *The New Yorker,* had been in the news. *The New Yorker* had run a cover with an editorial cartoon depicting Barack and Michelle Obama as Muslim terrorists. Cover got everyone riled up. It just gave Fiasco an impetus to read *King of the World* again.

After that, fiction, a new George Pelecanos novel.

Dude wrote some thrilling crime stories.

Also wrote for *The Wire* on HBO.

Fiasco had appeared in an episode. Not a speaking part. Cut a drug boy with a busted Heineken bottle, then exit stage left. It wasn't a stretch. Fiasco had done that and more when he was out there. Running the streets. Seemed like a million years ago.

MCing was all he cared about these days.

Rocking a crowd, writing that perfect lyric, getting his voice, his lyrics and his flow to come together and form the perfect song.

"Baby, when we gonna turn down these lights? I'm feeling some kind of way."

Toya.

Fiasco didn't even know her last name. And he didn't really care to find out, either.

He'd seen Toya for the first time at a club in Washington, D.C., first stop on the current tour. Then again in Baltimore. He got the hint in Norfolk, let her on the bus. He'd ride out with her until the tour was completed. Why not? She was the best-looking thing he'd seen in three cities. Best-looking thing he'd seen in some time. If he'd cared to delve, which he didn't, he'd have found out those curves had origins in the Dominican Republic and Puerto Rico. Pops was Dominican, Moms was a Puerto Rock.

And Toya was built like a brickhouse.

Fiasco went with that description, even though he'd never do to a brickhouse what he'd already done to Toya several times. Go to jail if he got caught doing that. Lewd and lascivious behavior. But whatever. Brickhouse Toya.

"You hear me, baby? I'm feeling some kind of way."

He wanted someone he could talk to about the general election.

The Sean Bell case.

The implosion of Sonny Liston's life, and the ascent of Ali's.

Fiasco couldn't help feeling pangs of disappointment, for not meeting Toya at the bank when he went to check on his mutual funds, for meeting her in those dark, smoky clubs instead. But it was what it was. Play on, player. Play on.

Toya's arms were around his neck. He looked up from his book. She was bare from top to waist. Had the most beautiful chest he'd ever seen. Couldn't deny that. He went ahead and closed the book. Killed the lights with a clap of his hands.

"Drunk ass!" Toya fumed. "The devil is alive. And you need Jesus."

Toya brought God into it, though the last time she'd been to church Moses was probably on the deacon's board. She was aggravated because an inebriated sister stepped out of the club, on wobbly legs, and proceeded to bump into her. Fiasco paid it no mind. He hadn't even seen the episode, was too busy gearing up for his performance. Could've been Toya's fault for all he knew. She'd had three Grey Goose and cranberry drinks on the bus herself. She certainly wasn't a nun.

No. None of that mattered. It was about his show.

Perform. Spit a gang of "hot sixteens" from his best-known songs, rock a couple of the new joints and keep it moving. Off to the next spot.

Touring was tough. Fiasco hated it.

That's why he'd gotten the bus. At least he'd get to rest his head in the same familiar spot every night. The road was lonely, though. Hence, Toya. But even with her, he couldn't deny the loneliness that clung to him like spiderwebs. Couldn't deny all that was missing.

Mya.

Her mostly.

And Eric. E.P. The li'l guy had gotten to him.

Fiasco didn't have many friends. None, really. Bunch of hangers-on, sycophants, yes-men. When the money dried up, so would their fake friendships.

That was okay, though.

It was what it was.

Fiasco considered himself lucky to know the drill.

"Can someone say 'hole in the wall'?" Toya gripped Fiasco's arm, pulled him close. He let her. "Your manager ain't jack," she barked. "He couldn't get you anything better than this? This is not no place for a star."

Not no.

Double negative.

Which meant the words cancelled each other, and in fact, Toya was saying this hole in the wall was just the place for a star. Fiasco frowned, accepted it. He didn't feel much like a star to begin with. Something dangerous was ticking in his blood. He recognized it, too, but was powerless to stop it.

Confidence. Swagger.

The things he counseled Eric on.

Must-haves.

Fiasco was losing them by the day.

Why? He couldn't put his finger on it. He blamed it on the rigors of traveling from state to state, day after day.

Whatever the cause, he didn't like what was happening to him.

He was on edge. Dangerous, he thought.

"I mean…" Toya let her voice trail off.

Fiasco understood. What could be said for the place?

The street was ghost-town quiet. The lights from the street cast an orange glow. Felt like a Western. The club was basically a storefront structure. Most expensive thing regarding the place was its sign. And the sign itself was cheaply made. Thin walls. Music bled out into the street. No nearby parking, so as people filed out, stumbling, they had to walk a ways to get to their cars. There wasn't a bouncer greeting patrons at the door. You just walked in and got to it.

Fiasco walked in through the front. He would have preferred not to have. But he couldn't locate a back door for talent.

"That's ten dollars, potna," a voice demanded. "The lady is free."

Toya was anything but free, Fiasco thought.

"I'm performing," he told the voice.

A little man moved from out of the shadows, removed a toothpick from his mouth, flashed a gold-toothed smile. "Crunk is DJing, potna."

"What's that?" Fiasco said.

Dude had on long black jean shorts and a dingy wife-beater. In a club. Let you know how low-rung the place was. Like Toya said. A hole in the wall. "DJ Crunk is spinning tonight, potna," the dude said. "Ain't no other performers."

Ain't no.

Another double negative.

And Fiasco was there to perform.

So this double negative, like Toya's, was appropriate.

They did have another performer.

"I was booked to perform here tonight," Fiasco said.

"By who?"

"My management team," Fiasco said. "U.N.I.T.Y. Management."

"And who 'sposed to be promoting, potna?"

Fiasco frowned. "Pimp Cup Entertainment."

"There your problem is, potna." Dude put the toothpick back in his mouth. "Big Bo over at Pimp Cup got into a situation. He been retained, what I heard."

"Situation?" Fiasco hesitated. "Retained?"

Dude nodded. "Young girl over in Fayetteville. Wa'n't but sixteen. But she looked to be twenty or more. 'Course that don't help the situation much, though. Big Bo forty plus. Least it would have been legal, though? Ya smell me?"

"We sure do...smell you," Toya said. "This is some BS."

Fiasco shushed her.

"I can see if Crunk mind getting you on the mic for a bit," the dude said. "No promises. Crunk can be ornery. You a rapper or singer?"

"Rapper."

"S'what I thought."

"What about my pay?" Fiasco asked.

Dude removed the toothpick again. "That I can't help you with. It'd be some exposure for you, though. Exposure worth more than money is. Ya smell me?"

Fiasco sighed. "I'm on tour, b. I've won a Grammy. Platinum every time I drop. I'm good with exposure."

Dude frowned. "What your name is?"

"Fiasco."

"Hmm. Got a funny accent. Talk like a New York n----."

"Jersey, actually."

"Nah. I wouldn't know you then. We don't mess with too many Jersey rappers down here. This the Dirty, potna."

"My crew is called Dirty Jersey," Fiasco said. "We the Dirty, too."

Dude wrinkled his nose. "Only one Dirty, potna. Dirty South, bay-bay."

Bay-bay. Baby.

He had a funny accent, far as Fiasco was concerned.

"Yeah, boi," the dude went on, "ain't nobody Dirty like us."

"You get no argument from me," Toya said.

Fiasco shushed her yet again.

"We gotta figure something out, potna," he said. "We drove all this way. I've got expenses. Gas alone is ridiculous."

"I don't know what to tell you, potna. I really don't."

"Get Tone on the cell immediately," Toya told Fiasco.

Tone. Fiasco's tour manager. Booker. Whatever.

Tone should've been with them handling these kinds of problems, but wasn't.

It was up to Tone to handle this mess. Toya was right.

But Fiasco didn't like it that she was so deep in his matters. His fault, though. Just 'cause her bedroom game was so on point. That's how men got messed up. Dropped the ball. Took their eyes off the ball. Lost in the game. Fiasco would have to do something about Toya. Soon.

He needed Mya around to keep everything square.

Fiasco headed back for the bus without another word, Toya calling for him. He ignored her.

"Sales been almost nonexistent outside of the Tri-State area. New York is okay. Jersey's fine, of course. Matter of fact, we're struggling in Connecticut. So even the Tri-State isn't holding us down."

"Tone, I traveled to this club for nothing," Fiasco said.

"And I'm sorry. I'll make sure heads roll for that. Our insurance will cover most of the costs. But we're not really in a position of power now, Fiasco. Understand what I'm saying?"

Fiasco fell back against a seat, rubbed his temples. "What we scan last week?"

The pause on the line made Fiasco think they'd been disconnected. "Tone?"

"Yeah?"

"What we scan last week, b?"

"Little under ten thou."

"What?" Fiasco shot up. "You sure?"

"Yeah. Positive. If we can limp our way to gold that would help with some of these bookings."

Gold. Five hundred thousand sales.

Fiasco had always been a platinum rapper. Always. A mil, solid.

"How far we got until we reach gold?" Fiasco asked.

Tone hesitated. "Halfway there."

Damn. Two hundred fifty thousand albums sold so far, that's it.

Album had been out eight weeks.

Sales had tapered off considerably. It would take a miracle to go gold. Gold.

"This is ridiculous," Fiasco said. "I've never sold so little."

"Times have changed. Consumers aren't spending money on albums. They downloading music for free. Or they bypass music all together. Gas prices are through the roof."

"Lil' Wayne did a million sales his first week," Fiasco said. "It can be done."

Tone put it out there. Broke it down to its very last compound.

"You ain't Lil' Wayne, Fiasco. I'm sorry, bro."

"Aight, Tone. One."

He hung up before Tone's hollow pep talk.

Confidence. Swagger.

Gone.

chapter 7

Kenya

"'LOVE does not begin or end the way we seem to think it does. Love is a battle, love is war; love is a growing up.'"

Lark and her quotes.

"Who dat?" I ask.

"James Baldwin."

I nod. "Cool."

Kewl.

"That's all you're gonna say?"

"What do you want me to say?"

Lark sighs, shakes her head, props her hand on her hip.

Frustrated with me.

"Look...Donnell's mother is sick." I pause, think about his mother. She was so weak, so broken, a shell of her usual self. I cried the moment I walked into her room.

Didn't stop until I left.

Donnell had tensed his jaw when he walked in, handed her the 7-Eleven bouquet of $9.99 roses, but didn't let any tears fall.

Being a strong man.

Until he left the room.

Out in the hall, he broke down.

I tried to console him as best as I could. Held him in a warm embrace for a few minutes.

Then he cleared his throat, gave me a courageous smile, thanked me and Lark for coming and walked off without another word.

I watched him go.

My heart heavy.

Burdened by everything that was happening.

"He doesn't need anything else to worry about," I tell Lark now. "Got enough on his plate. It would be selfish of me to stress him. He and I don't matter right now."

"Look," Lark says and points off into the distance.

We're in my Acura, idling in the parking lot of the hospital.

Been sitting here for close to twenty minutes talking to each other. Never made it out of the lot.

Affected by Donnell's moms's condition.

That put life into perspective. You never know what cards you're gonna get dealt.

"You see that, Ken?"

I frown as I look off in the direction of Lark's finger. "Thought he left," I say. "Where did he come from?"

Donnell emerges from the side of the building, settles down on a bench in front of the hospital, riffles through a handful of some kind of pamphlets. His forehead is lined in concentration.

"That boy needs you, Ken. Loves you. And you love him."

"Can't get over him going out with Melyssa Bryan," I whisper.

"You need to."

"Can't."

"So talk to him about it."

"Not a good time, Lark."

"Support him, Ken."

"Can't…Melyssa Bryan…what happened with Ricky… Sensitive about this kinda thing."

"Donnell ain't Ricky."

"Coulda fooled me. They all the same."

"You don't mean that."

"Don't I, though?"

"Donnell has been a good boyfriend," Lark says. "And you know it. Need I remind you that you broke it off with him?"

"Less than a week," I say. "He moves too fast for me. Never would have thought he'd move on so quickly. Nah, I'm good. Don't need anyone in my life like that."

"You finished?" Lark asks.

"Done."

"All that yin yang you talking doesn't move me, Ken. People make mistakes. The way you talk, you'd think you never even heard of a boy named JaMarcus."

"Low blow, Lark. Real low blow."

"Talk to Donnell about it, about your feelings. I'm sure he can explain why he did it."

"Nothing to talk about. Leave it alone."

"Ken, if you don't—"

I cut my homegirl off. "Leave it alone or get out of my car and walk your ass home."

I regret that immediately.

Too emotional.

Lark's lip quivers, eyes get glassy. "Just trying to help you, Ken. Don't wanna see you so unhappy."

My lip quivers, too.

Eyes glassy also.

"I know, Lark. I'm sorry. Shouldn't have yelled like that. My nerves are frayed."

"If you don't know life is short after seeing his moms..." She doesn't finish.

Doesn't have to.

I get it.

Uncomfortable as the situation might be, I can't let it ride like this.

"You're right. Gonna go talk to him. I'll try not to be long. Cool?"

Kewl.

"Worse comes to worse I'll walk my ass home." Smiles to reassure me.

"Sorry again."

"Go fix it wit your man."

I ease out of the Acura, softly, shut the door. Brush off my clothes, clear my throat, start walking.

Donnell's no more than a hundred feet away.

Feels like a hundred miles.

I become aware of my heartbeat as I walk toward him.

A drum beats in my chest.

Bangs…loudly.

"Donnell?"

He looks up from his pamphlet, sees me, at first is confused by my sudden appearance and then smiles. "Kenya? What are you doing here?"

I bite my lip, fidget in place. "Never left. See you didn't, either."

Donnell shakes his head. "Took a walk around the grounds. I had to clear my head somehow." He holds up a pamphlet, waves it. "Was just sitting here now educating myself. There's a lot I don't know about…about strokes."

Stroke pamphlets are in his hands, lots of 'em.

"That's good. Knowledge is power."

"Wanna thank you again for coming in with me. That was tough up there. Don't think I could've done it on my own."

"It was nothing."

"Nah, it was a lot. Meant a lot."

"Well, you mean a lot to me. It's the least I could do."

Donnell nods several times. Doesn't say anything.

He's too good of a dude to point out that I dumped him, and that doesn't jibe with me saying he means a lot to me. Inside I wince at the statement. It was a poor one. Sounds disingenuous, considering how I've treated him. Too bad life doesn't allow do-overs, doesn't allow you to take back what you regret.

Donnell sits back against the bench, looks away from me. "Don't know how we got here, Kenya."

I want him to call me YaYa.

"Me, either," I say.

Donnell shoots up suddenly, pockets the pamphlets, squares his shoulders. "You wanna grab a bite to eat? Some things I'd like to talk to you about."

"I need to drop Lark off."

"I'll follow you."

"You up to talking about...us?"

Donnell nods. "Get my mind off..." He doesn't finish.

"I went out with Melyssa Bryan."

I stop chewing my shrimp and pasta, wipe my mouth and sit back in my seat.

We're in Ruby Tuesday.

The restaurant is semidark, which matches my mood. That's the one good thing.

"Kenya."

"I know, Donnell. Heard about it."

He knits his brows. "You did?"

"News travels fast."

"I guess. And we're not even in school or anything. I could see then."

"Lot of haters, Donnell. Jealous of what we had. They were happy it happened. They couldn't wait to tell it. Somebody told Lark and..." Telling Lark meant everyone within a thirty-mile radius would know. I don't have to say that to Donnell. He knows how Lark is. Knows her reputation for having a mouth is rivaled only by folks on the radio or something. Wendy Williams.

Our business is in the streets. Heavy.

Donnell groans. "I'm sorry, Kenya."

I frown. A week ago I wouldn't have.

But now, hearing him say my full name causes me pain.

It speaks to the dysfunction of our relationship.

It's dysfunctional because it's not functioning correctly.

My fault. I broke it. Put a cog in the machine.

I say the only thing that comes to mind. "I'm sorry, too."

"You didn't do anything," Donnell says.

"That's nice of you to say."

I wait for him to reply. "I've missed you," I say when he doesn't.

"It's been a long, hard week, Kenya."

Would've been nice if he said he missed me, too.

Guess he hasn't.

How could he, filling all of his free time with Melyssa Bryan?

I fight off that jealousy. "Did I ever thank you, Donnell?"

"For?"

"Helping me get through the…the thing with Mr. Alonzo."

"No," Donnell says. "You never did. But you didn't have to."

"Thank you."

"It was nothing." He pauses. "You mean a lot to me, Kenya."

That makes me smile. Same words I gave him, about visiting his moms, less than an hour ago.

"I shouldn't've broken up with you," I say. "That was a mistake."

"I thought about it a lot," Donnell says, "and came to understand why you did it. It hurts still, but I understand your reasoning."

"Explain it all to me, then. 'Cause I don't even understand."

And there it is. Not much, but some. A crumb of a smile on Donnell's face.

"Can we start all over?" I ask.

He looks at me, deep. "I don't know, Kenya. A lot has happened. Can we?"

"I'd like to."

"You know I'd like to."

I clear my throat. "How are you? My name's Kenya." I reach forward, offer my hand. Donnell takes it.

"Donnell," he says. "It's a pleasure to meet you, Kenya. Do you have a man?"

I tsk Donnell. "Got your second chance and still haven't learned. This is a marathon, not a sprint."

He'd fought so hard to get me. Tried too hard. Turned me off originally. But eventually he got me, won me over, made me fall in love with him. Stole my heart.

"My bad," Donnell says. "How about you tell me what you're into, Kenya?"

"You. I'm into you. Do you have a girl?"

And there it is. Not much, but some. A crumb of laughter on Donnell's lips. "What happened to this being a marathon and not a sprint?"

"Do as I say, not as I do."

"You sound like my moms." Donnell laughs, no sadness visible. "You're gonna make a great parent someday."

"Sure you're right. Our parents kill us with that double-standard stuff, don't they? They're so hard to understand sometimes."

Donnell nods. "My moms used to beat me and then tell me it hurt her more than me. Tenderized my butt like raw steak and then said that. I always wanted to say, 'I doubt it, Moms,' but I kept my mouth shut and just iced my butt."

"Riiight. Mama would beat me, tell me to shut up, then ask me a question. I wouldn't know whether to answer or not. So I'd stay quiet. Then she'd whip me for not answering her question."

Donnell's happy.

"My moms told me to be home by the time the streetlights came on," he says. "This one time something happened. Lights never did come on. I strolled in the house like I owned it...around eleven-thirty."

"Ooh. You got your butt beat."

Donnell smirks, shudders. "Did I ever. She whipped me with this big plastic clock off of the wall and told me I better know what time is."

I laugh. "She did not. You got jokes."

"But seriously. It was all love. Unconditional love."

"The best kind."

Donnell quiets. "That's how I love you, Kenya," he half whispers. "No matter what mistakes you make, or made, I'd go on loving you, YaYa."

YaYa.

My smile is like a hundred-watt bulb, I'm sure.

He clears his throat. "You love me the same?"

I don't hesitate.

"I think so. Try to."

I notice his shoulders ease, tension release. "What happened to us?" he asks. "Was a time we were tighter than handcuffs. I didn't see that breakup coming. That's what hurt more than anything. Made me feel foolish after I'd gone out and bought you all those gifts."

I shrug. "Don't know. I'm going away. You're gonna be here. Got scared. Scared of getting hurt. Figured things would happen, so…"

"You plus me equals better math. What you always say, YaYa. I was down with that."

YaYa.

That warms my insides.

"Was?" I ask.

"Still am."

We sit in silence for a bit.

Think about everything that's happened.

Where we've been.

What we've gone through.

Where we'd like to go.

At least, that's the things I think about.

"Wish I could erase the past few days," Donnell says.

I take both of Donnell's hands in mine. "I want to be with you again. I want to be your girl. Matter of fact, I don't feel like I ever stopped being your girl." JaMarcus is evidence of this. As much can be said about what didn't happen with him as what did.

"Kenya—"

I cut him off. Come at him the same way he's come at me in the past.

"Don't complicate it." Squeeze. "A simple yes or no, that's all I'm looking for." Squeeze. "And just so you know. I do hope for a yes." Squeeze, squeeze.

Donnell shakes his head, sighs. "Kenya."

"Donnell. A simple yes or no."

"Yes."

I release his hands. Kiss him. In the middle of Ruby Tuesday. I don't even care. "All right, then. We're together again. Where we belong."

"Where we belong," Donnell echoes.

But there's one last piece of unfinished business.

"You like her?" I ask.

"Who?"

I hunch my eyes.

Realization comes to Donnell's face.

"It's not about like," he says.

"Oh?"

"Need."

"Need?"

"Hate to admit it. I'm ashamed of myself. But yeah, Kenya, I needed what she gave me."

I furrow my brow. "I'm not following. What you mean?"

Donnell swallows. "Melyssa's about one thing. Everybody knows that. I was torn up over you. I wasn't thinking correctly. She came at me, and I fell for it. I feel terrible. And I'm not just saying that. I felt terrible right after. I wasn't very nice to her. Even though she's... Well, even she deserved better."

He says more, but I don't hear it.

My heart starts to pound with the force of a sledgehammer.

Hands are clammy all of a sudden.

Throat is dry as old newspaper.

I can feel an ache tapping at my temples. Soon the taps will be a migraine.

I'll be dry swallowing one of Mama's Maxalt tablets.

Donnell notices the physical something that's happening to me. "Kenya, are you all right?"

"Are you saying you had sex with Melyssa?"

Donnell frowns. "Didn't you know?"

I drop my head, let the male lead in this born-again soap opera of a relationship know that I didn't.

chapter 8

Eric

I had front row seats to a local production of *Diary of a Mad Black Woman,* starring my sister, Kenya.

"This is ridiculous!" she yelled. "Why do I have to drive them?"

We were in the kitchen. Kenya, me and Mama. A meeting of the Poseys. Our kitchen table was like the conference table in the office of some Fortune 500 company. Mama was CEO. And if she didn't like our contributions to the discussion, she took on the responsibilities of vice president, COO, Chairman of the board, majority shareholder and office headquarters' head janitor.

A democracy quickly became a dictatorship.

Mama hadn't answered Kenya's question.

That wasn't a good thing.

Meant the dynamics of the discussion were shifting.

Kenya was Condoleeza Rice, in a tête-à-tête with bin Laden, Castro and Kim Jong-il.

Mama was loving. But tough.

When it was all said and done, it wasn't smart to test her. Kenya was toeing the line. I felt responsible, so I attempted to save her. Safety be damned, I was going in.

"This conversation would probably be a whole lot more productive if we had some fried chicken and macaroni and cheese in us," I said.

"You trying to give me work, boy?" Mama asked.

Boy. When Mama called me *boy,* trouble was afoot.

"No, ma'am… I…I…I can cook it."

I'd never so much as boiled an egg. A slight problem.

"Eric, quiet," Mama said. "This has nothing to do with you anyway. I'm talking to your sister." She gave me her dictator smile. "But go ahead and get cooking. Fried chicken and mac and cheese sounds wonderful."

They were arguing over a ride for me.

I thought that made me relevant to the conversation. But I wasn't about to point that out to O*Mama* bin Laden.

"Of course a bowl of Frosted Flakes would hit the spot, too," I suggested.

Mama actually smiled. "Thought so. You know where the bowls are. Frosted Flakes are in the cabinet over the sink. Milk is in the fridge."

That was a dismissal.

Kenya was in it up to her neck, and there wasn't anything I could do for her.

She knew it, too.

"I'm just saying, Mama…" she said.

That weak defense made me wince.

I busied myself preparing my meal. Got the bowl from one cabinet. Got the cereal from the other, over the sink as Mama had said. A quart of milk from the fridge. Big spoon from a drawer. I was tempted to get a pan and some Crisco. Fry my cereal. Anything to keep busy and stay out of this particular family business.

Mama turned her attention back on Kenya. "My eyesight must be getting bad, Kenya."

Kenya frowned. "What are you talking about? Your eyesight is perfect."

"Can't be." Mama shook her head. Her acting skills

rivaled Angela Bassett's. "I could have sworn my name was on the check that was used to purchase your car. But I must've looked at it wrong."

"That's dirty, Mama," Kenya muttered. "I can't believe you would stoop to that. The car was a gift. You gave it to me out of love. I didn't know there were conditions involved."

"And your brother needs a ride," Mama said. "But you're acting real roach, young lady. Everything's a one-way street with you. You probably don't remember the commercials for those old Roach Motels. 'Roaches come in, but they don't come out.'"

"I have no idea what you're talking about," Kenya said. "I don't think you even do." She smirked. "This whole conversation is buffoonery."

I groaned. Closed my eyes. Prayed.

And dropped the cereal bowl.

"Eric," Mama said.

"Yes, Mama?"

"Excuse yourself."

"I was gonna fix this cereal.... I'm hungry."

Mama's gaze was trained on Kenya. She kept it there. Didn't take her eyes off my sister as she reached in her pocket and pulled out a ten-dollar bill. Didn't take her eyes off my sister as she stretched her hand in my direction. "Take this and get yourself something out, Eric. And go now. Don't want you here for this."

I scurried over, hand outstretched.

Kenya bumped me at the last moment, moved over to Mama, plastered on the biggest smile. "You mind if I take that for gas?" Mama didn't reply. "For when I drive my brother wherever he needs to go."

Kenya said "wherever" with boldface and italics.

She knew the deal, finally. Was kissing some major butt.

"You wouldn't care to discuss my buffoonery?" Mama asked.

Kenya shook her head vigorously.

I imagined her mouth was Sahara dry.

Hollywood, Mama's boyfriend, stepped in then. He had a habit of coming in on the tail end of our knock-down-drag-outs. If I didn't know better, I'd think it was planned.

"What all going on in here?" he asked.

Mama still had her eyes trained on Kenya. "My chile is about to go get five dollars' worth of gas for her car. Then she's gonna bring me back my change and drive her brother wherever he needs to go."

"Five dollars!" Kenya protested. "That ain't gonna get me—"

I bumped Kenya out of the way, carefully took the money from Mama's fingertips and then ushered my sister out of the kitchen by her elbow.

"I'm not in the mood for all this, Eric," she muttered.

"I just saved you. Hope you recognize that."

She looked back toward the kitchen, saw Mama at the table, cracking her knuckles like a mixed martial arts fighter. Kenya shuddered. "True dat. True dat."

"Just 'cause you're leaving doesn't mean you lose your mind. You won't even make it to Georgia if you keep up like this. Are you crazy?"

Kenya's eyes had a faraway look. "Got a lot on my mind, Eric. I was tripping."

"Seriously. Pull yourself together, girl. It was almost Operation Iraqi Freedom Two up in there."

"It is what it is. Where did you need to go?"

I smiled, popped my collar. "Got a double date with Benny. The girl I told you about. Endia. And Endia's friend, Tanya."

Kenya frowned. "Lovely. Teenage love."

It didn't sound sweet when she said it; I preferred Alicia Keys.

I was in the front seat next to Kenya. She hadn't said much of anything to me. She hadn't played the radio, hadn't gotten any calls on her cell. She hadn't made any, either. Ditto for text messages. That wasn't typical for Kenya; her and Verizon Wireless were on a first-name basis. It looked to me as if she was suddenly living in a bubble. I kept glancing over at her, trying to get some kind of read. Nothing shone on her face. It was etched in stone. I was worried about her, but didn't press.

Benny was in the backseat. My friend was the opposite of my sister. Giddy. Souped-up.

"You gotta love how things play out," he said. "I'm a have a banger seated on either side of me, E."

I turned sideways, shot him a glare. "One of those bangers is mine, Benny. And the other is my doing," I reminded him.

"Small details, E. Very small details."

"If you say so."

"I say so. It doesn't matter, though. Once I close the deal with shawty, I won't be feeling any pain."

"Talk like yourself, Benny."

"I am, E. Hate it or love it, the underdog's on top."

I rolled my eyes.

"Hey, E?'

"What?"

"Shawty betta be thick."

Kenya turned suddenly, glared at Benny. "Men. Must y'all all be dogs?"

Then she glared at me and repeated her refrain.

"Bow wow wow, yippee yo yippee yay."

"You're sickening, boy," Kenya said.

"If I didn't know better, Kenya, I'd think you had a *scrush* on me," Benny said.

Kenya frowned. "Scrush?"

"A secret crush, shawty."

I laughed.

Kenya didn't.

I was glad she'd finally spoken, but something was bothering her.

Something more than having to chauffeur me and my friends was causing her angst.

Her eyes were moist.

Kenya, crying.

I couldn't imagine that.

And worse, there was nothing I could do about it.

We'd made it to Endia's house.

Endia's house was medium to large, with a brick face and stucco siding, on a quiet, tree-lined street. But she was the story. When we pulled up she was waiting on her porch, looking beautiful and stylish. She wore a chiffon dress, accessorized with a leather belt, and suede ankle booties on her feet. I suddenly felt underdressed in my jeans and T-shirt. But I had swagger for days. I'd be okay.

Tanya stood beside Endia. I was pleasantly surprised. She was sweet, too.

Funky, in a fur-trimmed top and bottom, with knee-high boots.

Benny was in jeans and a T-shirt, as well. But missing my swag, no matter how hard he tried.

I was slightly worried how everything would play out.

"Damn, E. Never knew you had jungle fever. Ol' girl is fine, though."

That set me at ease. "Benny, the white girl is your date," I said.

He hesitated. "Aight, aight. I can make that work."

"You're a fool. Don't embarrass me. Don't make me regret setting this up."

"My name's Ben…and I put work in."

"Lawd, Lawd, Lawd. No rhyming, Benny. Please."

Endia was making her way toward the car. The closer she got, the better she looked. I realized just how beautiful she was. Suddenly my palms were sweaty, mouth dry. No time to get nervous. No time to lose my swag. I quickly shook the feeling off. Damn! Endia really was fly. I got out to meet up with her.

We reached one another on the walkway, the halfway point between her house and Kenya's Acura.

"This is my homegirl, Tanya," she said.

I gave Endia a small hug, and then addressed her girlfriend. "Nice to meet you, Tanya," I said and shook her hand.

"You, too, E," Tanya said.

That brought out a smile on my face. Endia had been talking about me, a very good sign.

Tanya craned her head, nodded over my shoulder. "That your boy?"

I looked back. Benny was still seated in the back of Kenya's Acura. He sat reclined, one arm up on the rest, nodding his head and licking his lips. That was his cool pose. I was more disturbed by it than I could ever convey in words.

I turned back to Tanya, a sheepish smile on my face. "He's..."

"Cute," she finished.

"Say what?"

"He's cute," Tanya repeated. "I was worried. But it looks like things will work out."

"You wear contacts?" I asked.

She frowned. "No. Why?"

Cute.

Benny.

I couldn't form my mouth to say another word.

Instead, I just ushered the girls to Kenya's car.

I introduced Kenya to the girls, hoping the infusion of femininity in the car would move my sister out of her deep funk. Kenya gave Endia and Tanya a quick nod, but remained silent. Then I introduced Benny to the girls. Shockingly, Mr. Big Stuff was silent, too. Mouth suddenly wouldn't work.

Cute and mute.

Fiasco wasn't the only one with skills. I could rhyme, too.

"Where to?" Kenya asked.

If I hadn't been in the front seat, I wouldn't've heard her.

She spoke in barely a whisper. Didn't seem to have the energy to even drive.

"You sure you're okay?" I asked.

"Just great," she said and pulled away from the curb.

chapter 9

Kenya

I don't even know how I got here, standing outside my homegirl Lark's apartment.

It's rare for me to come by her place, even though she lives just four blocks from where I do. There's too much drama for me over this way, though. Lark lives on the third floor. And you've gotta hoof it up the stairs. Elevator's a death trap. And her stairwell's busier than a lot of dance clubs. A good-looking girl like myself is gonna get hit up on every level. First floor, bunch of wannabe thugs with no hair on their chests, dribbling one basketball between them, the ball damn near flat. Second floor, the building bum, vagrant, whatever you want to call him. You can't tell the dude he ain't fine. He tries game on every lady that passes by. His name is Two Cups. They call him that 'cause he keeps two beggar cups in front of him on the landing. Cups are filled with dirty pennies. Most of the people in the building are only a paycheck away from needing beggar cups themselves. Third floor, a Reggie Bush-looking dude with a red bandana tucked in the back pocket of his baggy jeans. A real thug, unlike the wannabes on the first floor.

No, thank you.

I ain't trying to be with a dude rocking colors, or any of them for that matter.

I know about all of these characters from the few times I've been here before. The faces never change, and neither do their positions in the building. I'm sure they approached me today. But I don't remember 'em. Just know I'm outside Lark's door. I must've gotten here by osmosis. Things are that bad for me.

I knock.

The door pops open; chain isn't released, though.

Lark peeks her head out. "What are you doing here?"

"I've got issues," I say.

"This is true. Been that way a long time. This warranted a visit?"

"Lark, please."

Her voice softens. "Why didn't you call?"

I frown. Eye her. The friendship that usually exists between us isn't present. She hasn't said my name once. Talking to me like I'm trying to palm off *Watchtowers* on her or something. Like I'm trying to sell her something she isn't buying.

"My bad, Lark," I say. "I didn't mean to bother you. I'll go."

I turn to leave, hear the chain release and the door open, quick footsteps, then feel Lark's hand on my shoulder. I don't turn to face her. Don't want her to see the start of tears forming in my eyes or the tremble of my jaw. "Whoa, whoa," Lark says. "Holeup, Ken."

"Wassup." I'm emotional. My feelings are hurt.

"I'll meet you downstairs in a minute."

"Don't worry about it, Lark. I'm kewl."

Kewl.

"Come on, Ken. I'm sorry. You caught me off guard. I'll be down in a minute."

I wipe my eyes with the back of my hand. Take a deep breath. "Okay. Thanks."

"What are friends for?"

"The tough moments."

"Exactly."

"Eric's little girlfriend is fly," I say.

"Shuuuuuut up!" Lark shouts. "He's got a girlfriend?"

"A li'l cutie. I might be overstating it about her being his girlfriend. But they're kicking it. I just dropped them off at the movies."

"Good for him."

"There's more."

"What's that?"

"It's a double date."

"Double date?"

"Eric's li'l girlfriend brought along her friend. And you're not gonna believe who Eric brought."

Lark clutches my arm. "Don't tell me he's kickin' it with Crash again?"

Crash is a man-child I went to school with. One of Eric's so-called friends. Fair-weather friend, at best. A bully to the *nth* degree. There was a time Eric was seriously under Crash's thumb. Like he was hypnotized or something. And Crash never returned the love. In fact, he beat my brother up last year. Eric's most humiliating moment in a year of humiliating moments. Then Eric met Fiasco. And everything changed. A new Eric emerged. E, as he likes to be called. Top of the food chain.

Swagger.

My brother had it now.

"Nope," I tell Lark. "Definitely not Crash. But good guess."

Lark puts a finger to her lip, taps it. "Can't think of anyone Eric is tough with. Other than that goofy-ass Benny."

"Da Da," I say.

"Shut up."

"Yup." I nod. "And Benny's girl was fly, too."

"Damn."

"And she was feeling that boy."

"Jean Claude Van Damn!"

"S'what I said."

Lark takes in a breath, shakes her head. "Well, this is all very interesting but not what you came over here for. So wassup?"

Count on my homegirl to get to the nitty-gritty.

I'm sitting on one of the green benches in front of Lark's building. Lark's standing. I look across the way. Girls playing double Dutch in the middle of the street. Mexican boys kicking a soccer ball around on the basketball courts across the way. Some old folks sitting in lawn chairs, gossiping. Lots of activity. Everybody into something.

"Donnell," I say.

"What a surprise," Lark says. "What he do now?"

"I'm not sure about the long-distance setup."

Lark nods. "I feel you. Donovan and I have the same issues."

Donovan wasn't going away to school. He was already working for his father's landscaping business. And he promised Lark he'd take classes at the local community college during down season in his father's business.

"Not quite the same, Lark. Trust me on that."

"Exactly the same," Lark says. "You have to set parameters. That's what we did. Donovan's idea, too."

"Parameters?"

"Yeah, Ken. Rules to live by. You'll crash and burn without them. Long-distance relationships are tough. Gotta have parameters."

"Like?"

Lark starts ticking them off on her fingers.

"We have to communicate a minimum of twice per day. One can be a text, e-mail, whatever. But one has to be live. Have to hear one another's voice."

"Agreed."

"Even if I'm stressed and gotta pull an all-nighter studying," she goes on, "I have to at least call him and speak for a few. That establishes that I am 'sugar sweet for he.'"

"'Sugar sweet for he?'"

Lark smiles. "Yeah. My baby."

Her Jamaican lover boy.

I'm not mad at her.

Do you. That's my motto.

"What else?" I say.

"If by chance I do see something else I want to get into, it's a must I'm honest about it."

"He's following the same guideline?"

"Of course. That's a must."

"Agreed, then."

"Feelings will get hurt regardless," Lark says, "but there is some comfort in the honesty."

"No doubt." I shift on the bench, very interested. "What else you got?"

"We're not gonna let more than six weeks pass by without seeing one another. So either he comes south or I come north every month and a half."

"Who's footing those bills?"

Lark smiles. "He's working. He volunteered."

"You got a keeper there, girl."

"Yeah, we're lucky, Ken."

We're lucky.

If only she knew.

I remember the time when I thought I was lucky to have Donnell's love.

Then I learned how fleeting it was.

He treated me like just some girl.

Worse, he acted like just some guy.

"So you see, Ken, it's all very manageable," Lark says.

"I don't disagree. It is manageable."

"Without a doubt."

"Just not for me."

"What?"

"Nothing." I wave her off.

"Something. Why are you giving off such a negative vibe?"

"Angry," I admit.

"I can see that. You look like La Toya that time…" I give

Lark a look that pauses her. "You don't want to hear anything about the Jacksons right about now," she says.

I shake my head. "Or ever."

"Sorry," she says.

I smile despite my heartbreak. "No prob, girl."

"So what's up, Ken? What am I missing?"

"Got other issues with Donnell that you don't have with Donovan. At least I hope you don't."

"Okay. Tell me. You're spoon-feeding me. That can't be good."

"It's not."

"Okay," she says.

I take a deep breath. "Your man didn't sleep with Melyssa Bryan."

"We need to get together," I say into my cell.

"Okay."

"Discuss some parameters if we're going to stay together."

"Parameters?" Donnell echoes. "If? Thought we'd settled that."

"If," I reply.

"I told you I was sorry, YaYa."

"That and a token can get me a ride on the bus."

"You are your brother's sister," Donnell laughs. "Sounds like something Eric would say."

"Don't make light of this, Donnell."

He regroups. "I'm sorry. Okay. When do you want to get together?"

"Gotta pick up my brother and his friends. I'll call you when I've dropped them off."

"Aight," Donnell says. "Call me when you get home. I'll swing by and get you. We can go to the park and talk."

"No. I'll meet you at the park. I'll drive myself."

"Why waste the gas? I'll swing by and get you."

"It might be the last conversation we ever have. Better this way," I say and disconnect the call.

chapter 10

Eric

Diary *of a Mad Black Woman* was still playing. Kenya was still in the lead. We were parked outside of Benny's house. Kenya and I were sitting in her Acura, Benny and the girls chilling out on his porch, waiting on me. The movies had gone well, and we'd had a good time walking around the mall, cracking jokes and hating on people we passed by. So I had talked Endia and Tanya into continuing our date at Benny's place. I suggested punch and video games, or a movie DVD, if they weren't *movied* out, in the plush comfort of Benny's den. I had to take charge; Benny was still mostly silent around the girls. I'd rib him about that for the rest of our lives, or at least until we were old enough to collect social security. Mr. Cool Stuff wasn't so cool with two pretty females around.

Despite Benny's lost tongue, Endia and Tanya were more than happy to keep the date rolling.

They couldn't get enough of us.

That was a good sign.

Almost everything was right with my world.

Almost.

Kenya didn't want to leave me, even though I assured her Benny's father would drop us all home. I was surprised by my sister's concern. It actually warmed my heart. Wasn't like her. I waited patiently for the other shoe to fall.

"You better let Mama know this wasn't my idea, Eric," Kenya said.

"E," I said.

"Whatever, boy. Just let Mama know I didn't have anything to do with this. Everything I'm going through, I don't need her on my butt."

Suddenly I felt foolish. Kenya wasn't concerned about me. It was about self-preservation. She was on some CYA. Cover your assets. Know what I mean?

"I'm gonna tell Mama you dumped us at Benny's door and peeled out of here like a bat out of hell," I said. "Bat out of hell" was one of Mama's sayings. That extra touch would really make an impression. "I'll say you left four teens with raging hormones alone in a big house by ourselves for hours," I continued. "You knew Benny's father was out and wouldn't be back for a while. I'll tell her a lot jumped off with the girls…but what happens at Benny's house stays at Benny's house."

I was kidding.

I wasn't about to tell any of that to Mama.

I was in good spirits, had jokes.

I thought myself so clever until I noticed tears spring in Kenya's eyes. Damn. This was serious. The other shoe had fallen, and I was the gum on the bottom of it. I touched my sister's knee. "My bad, Kenya…. I was joking."

She waved me off.

I rolled down my window, yelled to Benny and the girls. "You guys go ahead. I'll be there in a minute."

Benny's eyes widened, and I could see his Adam's apple protrude. "Hurry up, Eric," he managed. "We'll be in the den."

I nodded and turned back to my sister. Nervous. I wasn't used to Kenya showing weakness. Wasn't comfortable with the role of strong sibling. But obviously something had weakened Kenya, and I had to be strong for her, had to support her, encourage her through whatever tribulation was dogging her. My stomach felt like I was on a roller coaster. I forced a smile. "*They'll be in the den*. Ain't that something? An extra room to play around in. We've got a den, too. It's called my bedroom."

Kenya didn't respond.

"How do you make holy water?" I asked.

Nothing from my sister.

"Boil the hell out of it."

Kenya sobbed softly, gripped the steering wheel so tightly her knuckles pinked.

I swallowed. "What flower name would you give for the thing between your nose and chin?"

Nothing.

"Tulips."

I laughed lightly.

Kenya's expression didn't change. My jokes hadn't eased the tension.

I sighed. "Tell me what's up."

It took her a while. "Everything is all messed up, Eric."

She fell into my arms before I could respond. Another rare thing. I could feel her warm tears raining on my shirt. I patted her back, tried to offer her some comfort.

"Can't be that bad, Kenya."

"It is."

"Problem with school? You can't go or something?"

She shook her head against my chest.

Wasn't very vocal.

I'd have to guess her issue.

"Lark? Are y'all fighting or something?"

Another shake of the head.

"Donnell?"

She pulled away from me, sat up, board stiff. I'd finally hit pay dirt.

"What happened with Donnell?" I asked.

She sneered, said something I couldn't make out.

"Repeat that. Didn't hear you."

"Melyssa Bryan," Kenya blurted out. "She happened."

"Damn."

I couldn't think of anything else to say. Didn't have to even ask Kenya what exactly happened between Donnell and Melyssa Bryan. Melyssa's reputation was clear.

The gift that keeps on giving.

That's something everyone said about her.

"What are you going to do, Kenya?"

My sister shook her head, sighed. She looked like a world of weight was on her shoulders. Worse, she looked like she couldn't support it. "Don't know," she said. "Have no idea. I have to figure something out, but the well is dry."

I thought of every good piece of advice I could offer.

This was my chance to transcend our relationship, become more to her than just a little brother that embarrassed her half of the time and mortified her the other half.

Build on the strides we'd made in that room marked Private.

When we knocked out that monster, Alonzo.

Kenya tapped her steering wheel. "Well, let me get out of here."

My sister needed me. Think, Eric. Think.

"Aight, Kenya" was the best I could come up with. "If you need me, you know how to reach me."

I had to have more than that.

Kenya nodded.

I thought.

And thought some more.

Tried pulling something from deep within.

Something helpful.

Kenya was in obvious distress. I had to offer something else.

"And thanks for the ride," I said while I continued to think.

Again, she nodded, and then started the car.

I took that as my cue, hesitated briefly but got out.

I felt like a real punk, a complete failure, as I stood by the curb and watched my sister drive off.

My stomach rumbled.

My heart ached.

Kenya had needed me.

And I'd let her down.

Shake that thang
Let me touch that thang
I need that thang
I'm looooove…
With that thang

Yung Chit's mindless music leaked out of Benny's den. Chit, a rapper from the Dirty South somewhere, Tennessee or Mississippi or Georgia, I didn't even know where, was burning up the charts. "That Thang" was the most downloaded rap single in the country. As far as I was concerned Yung Chit was poison being fed intravenously into the vein of hip-hop. His lyrics led to a black pit of nothingness. Mindless. Dumb. Not the least bit thought-provoking.

Millions disagreed with me.

What did I know?

I shook off those thoughts, walked in Benny's den. It was like MTV up in there. Endia and Tanya were dancing smoothly in the center of the room. Endia moved like an ocean breeze, sexy as Ciara. Tanya's moves put me in mind of Shakira; she could really move her hips. Benny was off in a corner of the room, looking scared to death. I couldn't come up with a musician to compare him to. There wasn't one.

He stood, nursing a drink.

It looked like the hard stuff. Mountain Dew, I'd guess.

Some color came back to Benny's face when he saw me. He put down his drink and rushed over. "Hey, E," he said. "What took you so long?"

"Wasn't but a minute," I said. "Had to rap with my sister."

Benny turned the music down a notch. "Speaking of rap...did you ladies know my boy E here knows Fiasco?"

I hadn't told Endia.

Didn't want that celebrity friendship to be the basis of a relationship with her.

Benny was messing up my flow.

"What's he talking about, E?" Endia asked. "That's for real?"

I settled on a couch, Kenya on my mind. "Yeah. I know Fiasco," I admitted.

"You serious?" asked Tanya.

I nodded.

"If that's true, you get cool points, bro," she said.

Bro?

Was Benny rubbing off on her already?

Nope. Couldn't be. He hadn't said enough words to influence anyone.

"It's true," said Benny. "Matter of fact, E was in one of Fiasco's videos."

President of my fan club, Benny Sedgwick.

"Ooh. I would love to see that. Love, love, love to see that," Endia said before I could shut down any talk of the video.

Endia's eyes lit up.

Her voice held so much excitement.

Her mouth was turned up in a smile.

I loved her lips. Imagined myself kissing them.

"E's a little sensitive about the video, though," Benny said. "Doesn't like showing it. You have to have an executive order from the president to get him to show it."

Endia pouted.

Those lips. So full, so beautiful, so kissable.

"Go get your laptop," I told Benny. "Video's on YouTube."

Benny smiled. "Two steps ahead of you, E. I was hoping you'd say that." He nodded to a table in the corner. His Dell was on it. Wi-Fi Internet in full effect. Web browser already on YouTube. "Set it up in case one of these lovely young ladies could convince you to show it."

Now he wanted to talk.

I wanted him to shut up.

I walked over to the Dell laptop, typed in the search terms *Fiasco* and *unreleased video*. Six results; the video in question was third on the list. I clicked the link for the video. Adjusted the volume up. My stomach rumbled like it had earlier with Kenya.

Endia moved to my side, put her hand on my shoulder, watched the Dell monitor intently.

My stomach stopped rumbling.

"Wow," Endia said when the video ended.

"You were awesome, E," came from Tanya.

Benny just smiled like a proud papa.

Endia gripped my arm. "You're like...famous."

"Not hardly," I said.

"No. You are. That's so cool."

"I have an idea," Benny said.

I groaned.

"Why don't you call Fiasco, E? Put him on speaker so these ladies can have a word with him."

I shook my head. "No. No."

That'd be overstepping a boundary.

I felt Endia's grip tighten on my arm. "Oh my God. You should."

You'd think I was made with German engineering. I went from zero to sixty, from denying to dialing, in less than six seconds.

Fiasco picked up right away. "E."

In another time, without visions of Endia dancing in my head, I might have noticed the lack of feeling in my friend's voice. Might have heard the weariness. I didn't then, of course. Or didn't care. It was all about Endia.

I said, "Wassup, chief. I've got some friends here that wanted to talk to you."

"Some other time, E," Fiasco said.

"Got you on speakerphone," I admitted.

Fiasco hesitated. "What's good, friends?"

He was performing. That's what he did.

Endia and Tanya were too tongue-tied to offer more than "Hey."

"How's the tour going?" I asked.

"It's going." He grunted.

Endia's grip on my arm tightened even more.

Then she spoke.

Later, I'd wish she hadn't.

"Mr. Fiasco...?"

"Just Fiasco. Who dis?"

"Endia. Eric's girl. I mean, E's."

My heartbeat quickened. Mouth got dry. I felt dizzy.

Either I'd gotten food poisoning, or I was happy to hear Endia say she was my girl.

Fiasco's voice brightened for the first time during the conversation. "E's girl, huh?" he said.

"Yes, Mr. Fiasco. I mean, Fiasco."

"Endia...Endia," Fiasco said. "That name rings a bell. Hey, E, is this—?"

"Yes," I cut him off.

I could hear his smile through the phone line. It was that loud.

"What did you want to ask, Endia?" Fiasco said.

And then she said it.

"Do you know Yung Chit?"

There was silence on the line for a bit. "Yup," Fiasco said finally. "Sure do. He's the dude that sells out venues I can't even book. Sure do know him."

The bitterness in his voice couldn't be disguised.

"Cool," Endia said.

Totally clueless.

The first points I'd had to deduct from her tally.

That disappointed me.

"Aight, then," Fiasco said. "Be cool, friends. E, I'll get up."

"Bye," the girls screamed.

I don't even think he heard it, because I heard dial tone at the same time.

He was the second person I cared about but had let down that day.

I was batting oh-for-two.

Not good.

chapter 11

Kenya

I have a million concerns, a million questions for Donnell. But just to ease my mind, I'm going to ask him a million and one.

"How many times?"

"What?"

"How many times?"

"How many times?" is repeated back to me.

Frustrated, I look around, search for the source of the echo. We're not in a canyon. Not in some kind of echo chamber. We're in the park around the corner from my house. Birds chirp in the distance. The sun is slowly receding from a blue-orange sky. A white father wearing flip-flops, cargo shorts and a skater T-shirt pushes his daughter on a swing. A Latina mother wearing black Lycra stretch pants and a green T-shirt that hangs below her waist gleefully watches her baby master walking in a sandbox.

We're not in a canyon.

No need for an echo.

"How many times did you have sex with Melyssa Bryan, Donnell? And don't repeat my question back to me. I don't have time for this. If you want to act like the typical dude, I'll just leave."

"Once," he says. No certainty in his voice.

I narrow my eyes and watch him closely. He drops his head, looks at his feet, eyes blinking nonstop. I don't look at his hands. But I know he's wringing them. Women are lie detectors. We learn that early on, as girls. Have to have the ability to weed out the truth from lies if we're gonna deal with men. Men are liars, every last one of 'em. That realization makes me sad. I want this to be different.

Now I'm an echo.

"Once?" I say. "You're sure about that?"

"T-twice," Donnell stutters.

See. I'm not even stunned. I didn't want my third degree to yield another confession, but I was pretty sure it would. So sad.

"Twice?" I ask.

"Kenya," Donnell whines. "Damn."

I pay that no mind. "Twice? You're sure about that?"

This is torture.

"Twice," he says. "I'm positive."

"You're positive now. So how come your math was messed up the first time I asked? A simple enough question and you flubbed it."

"This is an uncomfortable conversation. I'm nervous."

I think of Lark. "No need to be scurred."

Don't know why that came out. I'm not feeling the least bit playful.

Truth is, I'm nervous, too.

"Easy for you to say," Donnell says. He winces, probably after noticing the change in my expression. Immediately regrets that comment. "I mean…you know."

"Easy, huh?" I say. "That what you think? Nothing is easy about this for me. Nothing."

He moves to me. Tries to touch me.

Can't.

Doesn't.

Unable.

I move away easily. Elusive.

Catch me if you can, I'm the Gingerbread Woman. This means, of course, I crumble.

Donnell stands five feet away from me. Feels like five miles to me. Probably five hundred miles to him. He's stuck on stupid, unsure of how to proceed.

That makes two of us.

I don't know how to proceed, either.

"So, twice... How many times did you two go out?" I ask.

"Once."

I hunch my eyes, cock my head, and place my hands on my hips. "Let me get this straight. You went out once? But had sex twice? That doesn't add up, Donnell."

"It is what it is."

I want to strangle him for that comment, but I don't. Have to remain calm, composed. Have to keep digging until I get the truth, the whole truth, and nothing but the truth. Unfortunately for Donnell, I'm his judge and jury, and possibly executioner. I hope not. But like he said, it is what it is. I'm down for whatever.

"Okay," I say. "Once. That isn't bad math again, is it?"

Donnell sighs. "Once, Kenya. We kicked it once."

"And y'all had sex twice?"

"Yes."

"Explain that one."

"You gotta be kidding."

I reposition my hands on my hips, tap my foot nervously. "Do I look like I'm kidding?"

"You look like I need to throw you some raw meat," Donnell says.

He tries to smile.

I don't.

Donnell sighs again.

It sounds like his last breath.

I've died a thousand times since I found about him and Melyssa Bryan.

He can die this once.

"I'm waiting," I say. "This better be good."

"Thought we settled all of this earlier, Kenya."

I frown. "You must be… I was too stunned earlier. I didn't ask you hardly anything about any of this. But I have a million unanswered questions now. And I have to ask them."

"I have to answer them?"

"No."

Donnell relaxes. His shoulders ease down, and the tension leaves his posture like air from a punctured tire.

"But if you don't…lose my number."

He eyes me. A funny thing happens.

His eyes turn hard.

Jaws set.

Lips protrude.

He's angry. Ready to turn this around, I bet. I wish he'd try. The anger is good, though. Makes us partners in our ire.

"You broke up with me, Kenya. Messed me up. I begged you to reconsider. You wouldn't hear me. So I went and made a mistake. While we weren't together. I repeat, we weren't together. That's a point you seem to be forgetting."

"If you're gonna take that defense, we can end the conversation right now."

His eyes turn harder.

Jaws set firmer.

Lips protrude farther.

Angrier.

"What you need to know? Fire away. Settle this…"

"Tell me how you ended up doing it twice with Melyssa Bryan in one day?"

Donnell runs his hands over his head. His chest heaves. He rubs his eyes. Shakes his head. "She hung out with me at my rest. My father had driven to Virginia to get my aunt to help him with…"

His mother.

For a brief moment I feel sadness.

This is all too much.

Donnell's going through enough.

I say "Forget this" in my mind, but not out loud. Color me selfish; I can understand, but I need to know, have to know.

Donnell clears his throat. "Melyssa hung with me watching movies. We were just relaxing. We watched a couple movies. Nothing was happening. Just two people hanging." He pauses, sighs. "I don't know, Kenya. I wasn't planning on anything happening. I know that sounds suspect, but it's true. We ended up messing around. I fell asleep right after. Restless sleep. I think I might have dreamed about you. No lie. And I'm not just saying that." He looks at me for some kind of hope. I give him none. He shakes his head, goes on. "When I woke up...things were happening again. That was all on her. She was on top of me."

Too much information.

Can my heart handle all of this?

"Twice," I say. "Once could be a mistake. Twice means no remorse."

Donnell's eyes widen. "No remorse? I told you how it happened."

"No remorse," I repeat. "Or remorse after the fact."

Donnell gives up. "I did what I did. I can't take it back. Wish I could, Kenya. I really do."

I ask a simple question.

But complex at the same time.

"Why?"

Donnell plops down where he was standing. We're on the incline of a grassy hill in the park. The children's playground sits at the foot of the hill. More than fifty feet separates us from the playing children. They're carefree.

Fifty feet away from us.

Fitting.

I'm eighteen.

A short distance from being a child.

This conversation is as grown-up as I've ever had.

"I've had so much going on, Kenya," Donnell says. "Mom sick. Dad stressed, sick himself. You going away. Breaking up with me." He frowns. Swallows, hard. Adam's apple looks like a buoy floating in rough, choppy waters. "I just wanted something easy. Something that wasn't stressful. Something just for me. Something that felt good."

They say the truth hurts.

And most can't handle the truth.

They're right on both fronts.

"Something that felt good?" I whisper.

Forever an echo.

Donnell nods slowly, purses his lips. "I'd be lying if I said it didn't. It's supposed to, Kenya."

The white father in the flip-flops, cargo shorts and skater T-shirt has his daughter on the slide now. The Hispanic mother in the black Lycra stretch pants and green T-shirt that hangs below her waist is off on a bench in a quiet corner of the playground, changing her baby's diaper. The chirps of the birds are farther away. The sun is starting to recede faster.

"I've never asked you how many girls you've been with," I say.

Donnell blinks.

Doesn't answer.

"Well? That was a question. I suggest you answer it."

Donnell frowns. "Love at first sight. That's some movie nonsense." He shakes his head. "But when I saw you for the first time, freshman year..."

I just look at him.

"I knew you were the one. I knew you were special."

I hug myself against the chill that travels up my spine. "I don't feel so special. As a matter of fact, I feel anything but special."

Donnell nods. "I know. And I'm sorry, Kenya."

"You haven't answered my question."

I vaguely remember conversations Mama had with my father when I was little. How he'd try to shift and change the course of Mama's probing questions. How she wouldn't let him get off track. I'll always remember those conversations. And as long as I'm in relationships, I'll have to. Men are manipulative. Manipulative liars. That's a sad but true reality. Ricky proved it. Donnell, he's proven it, too.

"You weren't listening, Kenya," Donnell says. "I did answer your question."

"I don't understand."

"I wanted my first time to be special. I wanted it to be with you."

My heartbeat starts to race.

I frown. "Are you saying…?"

"That I was a virgin?"

Somehow I nod.

"I was," Donnell says. "Melyssa's my first."

I've never run into a brick wall.

Never fallen off a steep cliff.

But now I know how it must feel.

I start to laugh.

Uncontrollably.

Wipe my eyes.

Donnell comes to me. "Kenya, what are you doing?"

Laughing.

Uncontrollably.

"I'm leaking eye water, baby," I say.

Lark's boyfriend, Donovan, would understand.

My tears flow like my laughter.

Neither will stop.

"You're scaring me, YaYa," Donnell says.

That snaps me out of it.

"Don't call me that," I bark. "Ever again."

"Kenya, I want to fix this," he says. "I need to fix this. I love you."

I shake my head. "This can't be fixed."

"Everything can be fixed."

"Not this," I repeat. "Not this."

"Gotta be something." Donnell's grasping for some hope.

I think of what can fix this.

Consider what can take away the pain and get us back on track.

"Only one thing can fix this, Donnell. Only one thing."

"Name it. I'll do anything."

"Make yourself a virgin again," I say.

Donnell's shoulders sag, his face drops. "Please don't get hung up on that, Kenya. It was a mistake. A big one, I know. But I'm human. I make mistakes, and I'm always gonna. The thing is whether I learn from my mistakes or not. Trust me on this, I have. So don't get hung up on this, please."

"First time is supposed to be special, because you'll remember it forever. So you'll remember Melyssa Bryan forever, Donnell. You know how that makes me feel?"

"Before I told you about it, you assumed I wasn't a virgin."

I shrug. Not my fault. "Loose lips sink ships."

Heard Mama say that.

Mama's here with me.

Need her for this very grown-up conversation. This very grown-up situation.

"YaYa."

"Told you don't call me that."

Donnell groans.

"You'll always remember Melyssa," I say. "Well, I also want you to remember this moment for the rest of your life."

"You think I won't?" The sound of burden in his voice lets me know he will.

He should've thought of that before he did it.

I start to walk off.

He calls me.

I turn, hands on hips. "What?"

"In my mind...when I was with her...it was really with you."

Somehow that doesn't help.

I leave him standing in the park with his regret.

Much later, as I reflect, I'll regret my next move.

But at the moment I'm moving on adrenaline.

I'm angry with Donnell.

No doubt.

But I'm just as angry, or more so even, with Melyssa Bryan. She took something special from me. Something more special than I ever knew. And there is no way I can get it back. She has to be held to account for that violation.

Jimmy Gents Convenience Store looms ahead of me.

You can get anything in Jimmy Gents. Milk, OJ, bread. Ten-cent candies: Mary Janes, jawbreakers, Blow Pops, tiny packs of Nerds. Mixtape CDs: a full representation of the *R*'s—Rap, R & B and Reggaeton. Faux leather belts. Do-rags. Strawberry shortcake ice cream bars. Everything. Jimmy Gents is the epicenter of the neighborhood. Been in the same spot since I was little. Will probably be there when I'm fully grown up with children of my own.

But it's what's across from Jimmy Gents rather than what's inside that occupies my mind.

Skintight blue jeans, a cutoff T-shirt with the word *Dime* emblazoned on the front, fake Steve Madden boots.

That's what that ho is wearing.

Melyssa Bryan.

She's on the corner, across from the store, with two other similarly dressed hoochie girls. Matter fact, they're worse than hoochie. They give hoochie a bad name.

A cigarette dangles from Melyssa's lips, plumes of smoke around her head.

Donnell isn't in the car with me. But I feel his presence. It's like he's riding shotgun in the passenger seat.

"There goes your future baby mama, Donnell," I say. "You do know how to pick 'em."

Can hear Donnell's labored breathing for a second.

Then I realize it's actually mine.

Breathing harder than P. Diddy after he ran the marathon. But I'm cool.

Kewl.

Also, hurt.

Angry.

But cool. Kewl.

Melyssa Bryan and her two girls don't have a care in the world. I eye Melyssa, cigarette dangling, doing a nasty dance right out in broad daylight. Her girls crack up, join in. All they need is a stripper pole. They're not far from that world.

I park in front of Jimmy Gents, right in front of a truck delivering goods to the corner market. I take a deep breath, then slide out of the Acura. Brush my damp hands on my pants. Take another deep breath. Start to walk toward Melyssa and her two girls. In my mind I give them stripper names: Cinnamon, Cashmere, Candy. The three Cs.

I don't have shackles on my feet, my hands aren't manacled, but you couldn't tell by my labored stroll. Donnell's actions have sentenced me to something. What, I don't know. But I'm prepared to do my time. I'm a stand-up female.

One of Melyssa's girls taps her, points in my direction. Not the least bit subtle. But that's how these gutter girls are. I don't expect more. Melyssa nods, continues coolly inhaling nicotine from her cigarette. Her other girl crosses her arms, plasters a scowl on her face. She must not know how close I am to scratching somebody's eyes out.

"Can I get a minute with you, Melyssa?" I ask when I reach them.

I address them all, though I'm only interested in one. Respect. Diplomacy.

"'Bout what trick?" asks the girl that tapped Melyssa.

I eye her. "I'm being pleasant. Tried to show you all respect. Why must you call me out of my name?"

"Come up here like you 'bout to do something," the same girl replies. "I wish you would."

"Somebody is fiddin' to get cut with that nonsense," the other girl says. "We don't play. We go all in, if necessary."

"I don't think that'll be necessary," I say.

"Whatever you say, *Paris,*" she snarls.

"Paris?"

"Hilton, bitch," she says. "Don't act like you don't know." She wrinkles her nose. "With your proper-talking ass. Straight-up white girl. You make me sick."

Looking back later, I'll realize this as the point I should have cut my losses and left. Before it got too emotional.

But I don't.

I turn to Melyssa. "I was hoping this wouldn't get *ignent*. But..."

Melyssa drops her cigarette, stomps it, eyes me. Doesn't say a word.

Trying to intimidate me, I guess.

"What's it gonna be?" I ask.

She eyes me some more, then head-nods toward my car. "Let's go chill over there. I'll give you your minute. But that's all you getting. I got places to be, and things to do."

"We be watching," one of her girls says.

I ignore that. Turn and head back toward my car, Melyssa on my heels. Behind me. My guard down. I realize that but keep up my confident walk. Don't want her to know I'm scared.

And I am.

When we reach my Acura, Melyssa touches the hood. "I ain't gonna front. I'm feelin' this."

"Don't get too attached. You've enjoyed enough of my...stuff."

"Ain't it the truth."

"Don't play me."

Melyssa smiles, looks at me, bats her eyes innocently. "And whatever might you have been referring to, about your stuff, Nigeria?"

"Kenya," I say.

Melyssa sneers. "Whatever. Knew it was one of them

wack-ass African countries with the crispy black n-----
running around with bones in their noses.”

"Self-hate," I say. "That's sad. Explains why you do the
things you do, though.”

Melyssa smirks, shakes her head. "You a trip, Britney.”

Britney.

A white girl's name.

Melyssa's idea of an insult. Paris, Britney, she can call me
what she wants. That doesn't hurt me.

"I really don't have any beef with you," I say.

"Good thing for you," Melyssa says. "'Cause I'd beat dat
ass.”

I nod. "Donnell screwed you and kept it moving. It is
what it is. I just have some questions. I was hoping you'd
answer 'em.”

Melyssa's eyes tighten. "You tryna play me, Libya?”

She's smarter than she lets on. Sad we have to dumb ourselves down to fit in. I've done that for as long as I can
remember. But no more. It ends today.

"You don't need me to play you, Melyssa," I say.

She doesn't catch the insult in my words. Or lets it go.

She waves a hand dismissively. "Don't catch feelings over
the Donnell thing. It was just a nut for the both of us.”

What a lady.

Donnell picked well.

"Can I ask my questions?" I ask.

"Fire away.”

I wince. Same thing Donnell said.

That hurts.

Any similarity between him and this hoodrat. Hurts.

"Was there ever any feelings between you two before you
hooked up?”

"Nope.”

"You sure?”

"Positive, Namibia. I mean, dude is cute and all. To
himself, don't bother nobody. Different than a lot of these

dudes. So I always noticed him. But Donnell ain't really my type when it all comes down to it. I like a dude with a li'l more hair on his… Well, you know. Tougher. Donnell's straight-up soft. I couldn't put up with that for too long."

I put aside my anger. That's my Donnell she's talking about. My Donnell.

Damn.

"How did you two end up…doing what you did, then?"

Melyssa shrugs. "You know how that goes. Things happened."

"Where did y'all hook up?"

"His crib. I'm sure he told you that."

I nod. "How many times?"

Melyssa smiles. "Gettin' all *CSI* with it. I ain't mad at ya. Double check those facts, girl."

CSI.

Wish Lark was with me.

"How many times?" I repeat.

"Twice." Melyssa smiles. "He was a little fast the first time." She sucks her teeth. "I ain't really get mines. So I went in again."

I swallow.

Do I even want these answers?

I do.

I must.

"You used protection?" I ask.

She sucks her teeth, frowns at me. "No glove, no love. I don't do that bareback. In these days, sheeit, that's crazy. That's some suicide shit right there."

So was promiscuity. But I wasn't about to point that out to her.

"You want to be with him?" I ask.

"Is you deaf? You heard what I said."

"Do you?"

"He's yours. I'm good."

"What did it all mean to you? Being with him?"

She sighs. "Nada. Not much, Condoleeza. Geesh."

"So you're not planning on making any more plays for him?"

She smiles. "It wasn't all that. I'm good. I need a twist, I got other connections, believe me."

I have one more question.

It may get my eyes scratched out.

"Don't you want more for yourself?" I ask.

She eyes me a moment. I notice a slight tremble in her frame. It lasts only a split second. She straightens her posture. "Nope. I'm good. Don't want for nothing." Pause. "We done, Ghana?"

"Yes."

Melyssa turns, walks away.

Sexy walk. I could see how a dude could get caught up.

She's pretty. Smarter than she lets on, like I said.

I watch her reach the other side of the street. She walks right past her two girls. They eye me angrily, then turn and follow down behind her. I disturbed something in Melyssa's thoughts. I'm disturbed, too. She's not interested in standing on the corner anymore.

Tears are in my eyes. I get in my Acura.

I pull away from the curb so emotional because of that brief conversation with Melyssa and my situation with Donnell that I don't look in my sideview mirror, don't see the delivery truck barreling down the street, hidden in my blindspot, until it smacks into me. The sound of metal pulling from metal and shattered glass lets me know a bad day just got worse.

"Pumpin' on my chest and I'm screamin'
I stop breathin', damn I see demons
Dear God, I wonder can ya save me
I can't die my Boo-Boo's 'bout to have my baby"
Snoop Dogg, "Murder Was the Case"

chapter 12

Fiasco

A journalist from *Vibe* magazine called. She wanted an interview with Fiasco. It had been a while since his music had gotten any national exposure. A small article buried in the *Source,* maybe three years before, was the last thing he even remembered. *Vibe* magazine wanted to rap with him? Of course Fiasco said yes. The writer wanted to talk about the current climate in hip-hop. A subject Fiasco had a lot of opinions on. He was game. More than game. He'd talk. Talk plenty.

He was good at that. Talking.

Talkin' crap, especially.

That had been Fiasco back in the day, a natural at it. And he could back it up, too, easily. Violence wasn't nothing but a thing for him, coming up in Camden. If he had a penny for every head he'd cracked, he wouldn't have to ever rock a mic again, he'd have himself a fortune. And girls. He'd gotten much love from the females 'cause he knew what to say to get them in a down-for-whatever mood. Talkin' crap. He had swagger in spades, everything 'bout him screamed that he was someone, a VIP. How he walked, the stylish way that he dressed, just his overall presence. The females couldn't say no.

And he couldn't stop himself from indulging.

He remembered one, as he sat reflecting with the *Vibe* journalist.

He'd been extra bold with her. He'd run up on her in a club, as usual.

"I can tell you ain't ever been loved good," he'd told her.

By loved he meant sexed.

"No?" She smiled. Intrigued. They all were.

"Uh-uh. You most definitely haven't."

"How ya figure?"

He'd nodded at her waist. "Your hips."

"What about 'em?" She'd looked down at herself, smoothed her skintight dress. Her body was *right*. What was he talking about? But he got her to thinking just the same. Maybe she needed to get herself a membership to Curves?

"You good and all that," he'd said. "Don't get me wrong. But your hips would be wider if a real n---- ever put it on you for sure." Talkin' crap. "You got that slim waist, a nice fatty, but your hips is lacking," Fiasco went on. "After I run through you'll be on some J-Lo-slash-Beyonce." *After* he'd said. Confidence. Swagger. And this was before he'd dropped a record. His first album was months away from release at that point.

"Is that so?" she'd said.

"No doubt."

"How I know you ain't just talking yap?"

"Real n----- do real things."

She'd eyed him, hard. "I must be crazy, but I'm considering this."

Fiasco smiled. "Coquetry then coitus."

Webster's Dictionary. He'd read the entire thing.

Every letter had a story with it.

"What's that?" the female asked. "Them words?"

"Flirting then...loving." He'd almost said the F-word, but edited himself. Keep it clean. He had her. No use messing it up by being too raw. Same principle he applied to his rhymes.

She nodded, impressed. "You got a vocabulary. What, you in college or something?"

The year 2000. The new millennium. He was twenty-one. Should have been graduating from Howard.

"Nah. I'm an MC," he'd said.

MC. Not a rapper. *MCs* were artful, intelligent, expert with words, lyrically nimble.

Rappers weren't necessarily on that level.

She'd frowned. "MC? What's that?"

"I spit. Rock the mic. Rhyme."

"A rapper?"

"Yeah," he said, though it pained him.

"I ain't ever seen you on MTV, BET," she said. Smiled, proud of herself, as if she'd gotten one off on him.

"You will. Finishing up my album now." Said it with a confidence that couldn't be denied. "By the way, what's your name?"

"Mona. You?"

"Fiasco."

"Your government?" she said.

"Fiasco's enough."

Mona appraised him, head to toe. Crisp white sneakers, looked like they were right out of the box. Designer jeans that lay down perfectly over the sneakers. Black hoodie. And not some Wal-Mart nonsense, either. The stitching let her know it was expensive material. He smelled good, too. *Cool Water,* she believed. She looked him in his eyes. They had an Asian slant to 'em, but he was definitely black. Put her in mind of Tyson Beckford. She licked her lips. "Fiasco the rapper. You any good?"

Instead of nodding, he demonstrated. "When we speak it's like vagina monologue/ you want what is mine as yours/ and that's a minor flaw/ but we could shine or soar/ or I could rhyme some more/ convincing / you with every word/ to walk with me out the door."

Off the top.

A freestyle.

Delivered with swagger, too.

Mona had gripped his hand and pulled him out of the club. Pulled him out. Their one-night stand lasted a couple of years. She'd been one of the better ones. Actually came to the studio as he was finishing up his album, offered her support as he recorded his word magic. Believed in him. Believed in him before he blew up.

Even Mya liked her.

And Mya didn't like any of 'em.

But Fiasco was wild, then. He didn't listen to Mya as much as he should have. One female wasn't enough. Destiny Broadnax replaced Mona. Actually, she overlapped with Mona, but whatever. Destiny was beautiful, and wounded. Her five-year-old son had gotten killed the year before. Gang mess. Right on the sidewalk in front of Destiny's mother's place. The little boy playing with some action figures. Cut down when some fools drove by and sprayed the block, thwat-thwat.

Wrong place, wrong time.

The experience had warped Destiny.

She didn't care about nothing; she went for it all.

Fiasco liked that; it reminded him of himself. He benefited from it. Destiny was down for whatever. He made sure "whatever" was usually an MC named Fiasco.

His second album had just dropped. A critical and commercial success. Write-ups in all the major mags. *Vibe*. The *Source*. A single getting heavy play on the urban stations. Nice little video on rotation on MTV, BET and VH1. His swagger was bigger than ever. The females loved him. Mona and Destiny had actually gotten in a fistfight over him. Destiny won. Wasn't a female anywhere that wouldn't throw down for a chance with Fiasco. He was a hot commodity with the females.

Dudes were another story.

Bunch of cats around his way were serious haters. He

stayed away from Camden as much as possible, but he wasn't a sellout Negro; he had to go back to the old neighborhood from time to time. Had to breathe that Camden air just to keep himself on point. Not that it helped with sales from where he really wanted them. It was cool the ladies liked his records, but he wanted the dudes to respect his flow, too. That was a lost cause. He didn't get love from dudes anywhere. They complained that his music was too soft. Eventually he moved his focus. Screw 'em. They didn't buy records anyway. The ladies did. And Fiasco had enough rugged nonsense in his life; why would he waste his energy spitting the same thing on a song? Let 'em hate.

He had fine-ass Destiny.

They got busy in motels most weekends he came home.

Didn't even speak during the week. Didn't really speak much in the motels, either.

But this one night, Destiny was in a talkative mood.

"How long were you in prison?" she asked.

Fiasco frowned. "Who said I was in prison?"

She'd glanced at him knowingly.

"A minute," he admitted. Little over a year, over some foolishness. He'd learned.

"Tell me about it," Destiny said.

Fiasco shook his head. "No, ma'am."

Destiny pouted. "Bet that'll help you sell records. Street cred."

Fiasco plopped down on the bed, started disrobing. "I'm keeping all of that quiet. I'm gonna sell records 'cause my flow is tight."

Destiny grunted.

"I've got skills," Fiasco said. "That'll prevail. Me getting locked up isn't relevant."

"Street cred," Destiny said a second time.

Fiasco frowned. "Suppose I should walk around talking about all the times I've been shot at, too?"

Destiny seemed to shrink away from him at the mention

of getting shot, dropped her eyes, got playful with her hands. He'd never seen her look shy like that before.

It turned him on.

"Come and get this Yao Ming," he said.

Destiny seemed uncertain, but she moved to him, dropped to her knees. Fiasco closed his eyes. Destiny worked his pants off. They were shackled around his ankles. He felt the coolness of the room when she dropped his boxers. "Tell me about prison," she said in a shaky voice.

On that again?

Fiasco kept his eyes closed. "A mistake. But I learned from it. Grew. I read the dictionary, cover to cover. Learned a lot of words."

"You learn a word for 'stay completely still,' n----?"

Fiasco felt more coolness. On his temple.

He opened his eyes.

Some strange dude stood beside him, gat resting on Fiasco's head.

"Move one inch," the dude growled, "and they'll have to wipe you off the walls."

It had gotten hot for Fiasco quick.

The air in the room was thick enough to spoon in a bowl. Fiasco wanted to wipe his brow. He didn't. Sweat beaded on his skin.

"Okay if I pull my boxers and pants up?" he said.

A click sound reverberated through the room. The release of the gun's safety. That meant no in gun talk. Fiasco spoke gun talk fluently. He left his boxers and pants around his ankles. Felt a tick in his blood.

Fiasco looked at the gunman. Big ugly dude. Had his hair pulled back in a ponytail so tight it Jet Li-ed his eyes. He was dressed head to toe in black. A worker bee.

"What's this about?" Fiasco asked.

He had his ideas, of course. Dude turns his burner on you only two things it could ever be about, really. Money. Or some female. Dudes acted tough and whatnot, but a female could get the baddest n---- twisted up in a second. Fiasco glanced over at Destiny. She stood stock-still in the corner of the room. Shocked, it seemed. It wasn't about her.

"I ain't hardly Bill Gates, son," Fiasco said.

"I've heard otherwise," said the Black Jet Li. "I want your ATM card. And your PIN."

"Don't even have—"

The gat pressed harder into Fiasco's temple, bit into his skin. "Don't lie, Fiasco. Don't even."

"I'm saying…" Fiasco searched his mind for something. "I can get you some money, though. But it'll take me a minute. I don't have it on hand like that."

The Black Jet Li backhanded him. "Don't play me. Destiny said your dumb ass keeps all your money in a savings account. And she said you be at the ATM several times a week."

Fiasco's head swam. He'd lost some of his sharpness since he'd started recording. Misread everything in this situation. He'd been set up.

He glanced at Destiny again, met her steely gaze. Something in her eyes said *I'm sorry*. Something in his return glance said *Eff you*. She turned away, trembled. Her eyes were moist. An actress. Playing a role. He'd fallen for her lines. And she'd betrayed him good.

"Wallet's in my right pocket," Fiasco said. "PIN is zero, zero, twenty-two, seventy-two."

No sooner had he said that than the gun went off.

Shot four times. Something he never mentioned in interviews. A media secret. Fiasco wasn't about to sell records off of his unfortunate past. Didn't want his destructive past life feeding the young and impressionable minds of his fans. Didn't want them buying CDs because they thought his past brushes with thuggery, getting shot and whatnot, was cool.

Getting shot wasn't cool.

Living was, though.

Living allowed him a second chance.

Allowed him to leave that life behind, focus solely on the music.

And he'd done that for the most part. He'd come close to selling his soul last year. Recorded a hard street record under the alias Murdaa. But at the last moment he scrapped that project. Just couldn't go through with it. The near tragedy with Alonzo and Eric's sister had refocused his mind. He made good music as Fiasco. Intelligent and thoughtful music. Uplifting music. The Murdaa record was reckless, a mistake he narrowly avoided. Mya was happy. One of the few times he made her happy last year. And his fans still had music. Fiasco. They still had a choice.

And they'd made it.

His album was tanking. Sales were thin as Calista Flockhart. Meanwhile, all these talent-challenged rappers were moving units. Yung Chit, a primary example. The Southern rapper's CD had come out around the same time as Fiasco's and was two times platinum already with no end in sight.

Two million in sales.

Everybody loved Yung Chit.

Even Eric's little girlfriend.

That bothered Fiasco. Really put him on edge.

And Yung Chit was everywhere. Constant reminders in front of Fiasco's face. Ubiquitous. One of the words Fiasco had learned. Yung Chit in magazines. On the radio. TV. Trumpeting the time *he'd* gotten shot as if that made him a better artist. As if taking bullets had increased his lyrical ability on the mic. It hadn't.

Fiasco had a choice now, too.

What was that saying? If you can't beat 'em, join 'em. Should he speak about his past? Talk about the shooting? Would it even help at this point? And did Fiasco want that kind of help?

The *Vibe* journalist sat forward in her seat, her recorder playing, interest in her eyes.

He'd told her the entire story up until the shots.

A Latina with sexy, large eyes, and a warm, winter-proof smile, not to mention a thick li'l athletic body. She flashed that smile, batted those sexy eyes. Fiasco felt her smooth fingers on his knee. Wasn't even sure how it had gotten there, she was so subtle.

Vida. That was her name.

"That is some story," Vida said. "You haven't told it before?"

He shook his head. "No. I haven't."

"Why not?"

"Focused on my craft. The art."

Vida nodded. "Congratulations on your newest release."

"Thanks," he said. "Congrats on a dud?"

"I have all of your songs downloaded in my iPod. There isn't a weak song on the entire CD."

That was something he could get behind. "Thanks. Glad to hear you feel that way. I worked hard on this album."

"It's evident," she gushed. "Nas famously said 'Hip-hop is dead' a few years back. How do you feel about that statement?"

"A lot of truth to it."

"Meaning?"

Fiasco shifted in his seat. "Meaning real music isn't getting made anymore. A bunch of jingles masquerading as songs."

Vida smiled again. "Your album is critically acclaimed, but according to SoundScan you've sold only 135,000 copies. Reconcile your sales with the artistry of your music."

She'd done her homework.

One hundred thirty-five thousand. Worse than he knew.

"It's disappointing. But I don't get enough spins on the radio. I don't get the interviews anymore. The young kids that buy the music are led like rats to cheese. They're influenced in what they buy. And I'm not the cheese anymore."

"Interesting." Vida's eyes glowed. So did her smile. "Why do you feel—in your words—you aren't the cheese?"

Fiasco shrugged. "I don't know." He did. Why avoid the truth? He cleared his throat. "The marketing of rappers has changed. It's about the backstory more than the music."

Vida laughed lightly. "That's the truth. A compelling backstory helps sell records. You haven't been arrested. Your name doesn't come up in anything negative. As opposed to, say, a Yung Chit. He's burning up the charts right now. He's been arrested, shot, everything. The critics aren't kind to his music, but it still sells. That boosts your theory, I'd say."

Yung Chit.

Everywhere.

Ubiquitous.

Fiasco wasn't letting Yung Chit steal another second of his shine.

He shifted in his seat again. "Dude doesn't make good music. Let's be real. But everybody is caught up in all the arrests and the shooting as if that means something. And Yung Chit harps on that because he knows his music isn't noteworthy."

Fiasco paused. This was the moment of truth.

"What's funny," he continued, "is I could have went that same route, but didn't. I think he's a fake thug, actually. Real thugs don't announce the shit on billboards. I could have done the same thing as him, but I wanted my music to be the focus, not the fact I'd gotten shot in a motel room with my pants down. And spent time in prison."

Vida's eyes widened. "Are you saying—?"

"That I've been shot? That I've been to jail? Yes. I told you *some* of my story, but not all of it. Let me keep it all the way real with you…"

Spanish music was playing softly on the restaurant's jukebox. The singer, a female with a voice like velvet, kept singing the same two words: *amor, corazon*. The musical backdrop consisted of guitar licks and what sounded like an accordion. A couple in the rear of the restaurant danced around a pool table. Lark didn't want to be there. But her father insisted. And you didn't tell Earl Edwards no.

"Heard the barbecue here is off the hook," Earl said.

Off the hook. Lark's father still thought he was young.

"Your father's talking to you," Honey said. "Answer him, girl."

Was he? Lark hadn't realized. "Oh yeah?"

Earl chuckled. "You weren't even listening. It's all good, princess. Your night, live it how you will." He paused, picked up his glass, took a swallow of the amber-colored liquid inside. "I'm getting faded."

Johnny Walker Black, Lark believed.

How embarrassing. Lark sighed as Honey fixed her gaze on her, eyes tight, jaws tense. A slap would have followed if they weren't in public. Honey was blaming Lark for her dad's drinking. Convoluted logic, but whatever.

"Thanks, Dad," Lark said. "I really appreciate this celebration."

Celebrating her leaving for school.

Earl waved her off. "Sure you do."

Honey's eyes tightened even more.

Lark's father swimming in the Johnny Walker.

It was bound to be a long, suffering evening for Lark.

Donovan had gone back to Jamaica with his parents to visit relatives. She wished he were here. She wished her parents would have let her bring Kenya.

Speaking of Kenya, she hadn't heard from her friend in hours. That was unusual. Lark pulled out her phone, kept it shielded under the table, sent Kenya a text message: I'm dying over here. Parents have me out for dinner. :(

Their dinner orders arrived.

Baby back ribs, a side of black beans, Carolina coleslaw made with apples, apple juice and cider vinegar. Same order for all three of them. Lark was in the mood for chicken. But her father had ordered. And you didn't tell Earl no.

Guy who served the food had blond dreadlocks, blue eyes, walked with a serious bop. Bob Marley mixed with Brad Pitt. Lark thought he was cute. She couldn't help but stare. The only good thing about the evening so far. She was at the point of noticing guys more than ever. Hormones in overdrive. Girls went through the same things boys went through in puberty. But how could you not notice this guy? Big and beefy, looked like he could have played linebacker for Nebraska and then moved on from there to the NFL. He'd ruptured his ACL rushing the quarterback, had his career cut short, came back to Jersey and opened up this quaint little restaurant. He wasn't just a waiter; he owned the joint.

Lark created a complete story around him.

Just looking at him opened the floodgates of her mind.

Flannel shirt, opened, a gray T-shirt under that, sleeves of the flannel shirt rolled up to his elbows. He wore a white apron over everything; it was covered in long, maroon squiggly stains. Barbecue sauce, Lark hoped. His blue jeans were torn in both legs, a hairy sunburned knee visible in his right pant's leg. He placed their food down before them, unsnapped linen napkins and dropped them on the table beside their plates. Lark noticed a bracelet of different color rubber bands wrapped around his thick right wrist. His hands were huge. He could have been a cornerback maybe?

Lark had to gather herself. Donovan was teaching her football, but she couldn't imagine he'd be happy she was using the new knowledge for this, fantasizing about some hot white man in a restaurant. She looked away from the blond dread, eyed her parents. Fantasy was better than reality, though.

The blond dread said "Rail up" after he'd settled their food in front of them.

Accent. Jamaican.

Oh boy!

God seriously had a sense of humor.

Lark's father rubbed his hands together and nodded. Dug in right away. Honey bowed her head and said a quick prayer. Hypocrite, Lark thought. At least her father didn't pretend to be friendly with the Lord.

The blond dread nodded at her father's empty glass. "More libations?"

Earl shook his head. "No thanks. But I will have another Johnny Walker Black." He cackled, found that so funny.

Dumb. Lark wondered how come she was so smart. Where did it come from?

Honey? Earl?

As Kenya would say, Oh hells no.

"I'll bring dat straightaway, nuh?"

Lark's stomach rumbled. For a second she'd thought, hoped, her father wouldn't get drunk. She wanted to tell Brad Pitt-slash-Bob Marley of how bad things got at the apartment when her father drank, but she couldn't. She hadn't even shared that knowledge with Kenya, her best friend. Best friend who wasn't returning her text messages. Three so far.

The blond dread paused, his blue eyes unblinking behind the curtain of nappy blond hair. His jaw muscles were tight, rippled his skin. He glanced at Honey. "You, ma'am?" She shook her head. Then he turned to Kenya. Didn't speak, asked with his eyes. Beautiful blue eyes. "No. I'm good," Lark said.

She wasn't.

He seemed to realize it, too.

His eyes stayed on her for several beats.

She noticed his Adam's apple, dancing in his throat.

He finally looked away, scooped up her father's empty glass. "Soon come." He stepped away, bopping, dreads flapping.

Lark snuck another text message to Kenya. This made four.

"A blond dread," Earl said. "Is that the Twilight Zone or what? Where's Rod Serling?"

"Who?" Lark said.

Earl chuckled. "Wow! I know something you don't know. Wow!"

"Whatever."

"Yeah, whatever," Earl barked. "Whatever. Whatever."

Honey laughed a nervous pitter. She knew her husband.

Knew he was teetering on the edge. Knew what that meant for her. Nothing nice.

Lark bit into her ribs. "Ribs are good, Daddy." They were.

Earl, neck deep in his own, grunted.

They ate in virtual silence. Food was good, better than good. Ribs tender. Barbecue sauce tangy and sweet. Black beans firm and flavorful, dusted with cheese. The non-mayo Carolina coleslaw top-notch. Earl grunted after every bite. Honey hummed every so often. Lark just ate.

And thought.

What was up with Kenya?

Lark was up to six messages. No reply.

"You never did say how that school visit went." Earl bit into his tender ribs; barbecue sauce dripped to his chin. He didn't bother wiping it away. His shirt looked like the blond dread's apron. Embarrassing. "You need to learn to share your experiences with your folks." Slurring.

"We just the piggy bank, Earl," Honey said. "Ain't you figured that out? Ain't no sharing with us."

Scholarships, scholarships, scholarships.

Part-time job, part-time job, part-time job.

How were they the piggy bank?

Lark was doing it on her own. Like with everything.

"It's nice," Lark said. "Sorry you guys couldn't visit with me."

"I bet you're sorry," Honey said.

Lark ignored her. "I'm thinking about joining a sorority."

Earl grinned. "Delta Alpha Sigma Phi Theta Beta Sigma Gamma. That's my princess."

Oh, he was definitely drunk.

"Kenya and I might join," Lark said.

"Following behind that girl on everything," Honey barked.

"She's my best friend."

"But you ain't no Kenya yourself. Sooner you learn that, the better."

"What's that supposed to mean, Mama?"

"What I said. You ain't no Kenya. That girl's beautiful and talented and…"

"…got a phat ass," Earl finished. "Not that I've noticed but a time or two or three."

Honey acted as if she hadn't heard that.

Lark bit her lip.

Honey smiled. "Don't worry about it, girl." Soft tone, as if she cared. "Everybody ain't meant to be special."

Lark wasn't even mad.

Kenya *was* special.

The best friend a girl could have.

But why wasn't she returning her texts?

Lark was worried.

The blond dread returned to clear their plates. He glanced at Lark briefly. She smiled. He looked away, launched right into business. The place offered two desserts only: apple pie or ice cream. Or, if they were truly ambitious, apple pie with a scoop of ice cream on top. If they wanted coffee, there was a Starbucks two blocks over. Keep it simple.

Nobody at the table wanted dessert.

"Best barbecue ever," Earl slurred to the blond dread.

"Sassafras and applewood."

"Come again?"

"The wood we use to cook-up on," the blond dread replied. "Makes it good, nuh?"

Earl nodded. "That's ups what's." His tongue was a weight.

The blond dread fixed his steel-blue eyes on Earl, brushed aside a handful of blond dreads. "Can I offer you some coffee?"

"Thought you didn't serve coffee?"

"My private own."

Earl waved him off. "I'm straight."

"I'm driving," Honey said.

"To hell you are."

"Earl, please…"

"To hell you are," he repeated.

Honey let it go.

"Long as the Pope pisses at the Vatican, I will be the man in my house," Earl slurred. He slammed his fist on the table, shook silverware, made the salt and pepper shakers dance, keep up beat with the Spanish woman singing about *amor* and *corazon*.

The blond dread stepped away.

That disappointed Lark.

She glanced at her cell phone again.

Nine messages.

Kenya, where are you?

The drive home had been uneventful. Not much happened. The real fireworks were when they first left the restaurant, getting Lark's father to hand over the keys. After some fight, he did. Now, the streets were dormant. It was an unseasonably cool evening. The hawk was actually out, keeping the criminal element at bay. Earl was asleep in the passenger seat. Honey drove carefully, had made one stop, at 7-Eleven. Bought a handful of items that would have been cheaper at the grocery store. And her lottery. Cash 5, Quick Picks.

Night had fallen hard, painted the sky black.

Honey pulled down the alley of their project building. One of her shortcuts. They were blocked. A Lincoln Continental, dark blue, late model. Out-of-state tags, Indiana. The car's brake lights were blinking like Christmas decorations.

Honey honked her horn. Nothing. "Go tell them to move," she told Lark. "I ain't got time for this."

Lark slid out of the car, took tentative steps toward the Lincoln. Brake lights were still blinking like crazy.

She moved to the driver's side, was about to tap on the window, but stopped abruptly. Inside, a middle-aged man's trousers were pooled at his ankles. A woman, crooked brunette wig on her head, was bobbing up and down in the man's lap. She wasn't bobbing for Granny Smiths, either. The man's head was thrown back against his headrest, his foot tapping the car's brakes unintentionally.

Lark stumbled backward.

Honey honked her horn again.

Lark stumbled a couple more steps.

Honey rolled down her window. "Girl, what you doing?" she yelled. "Tell them to move."

Lark stumbled down the alley.

In the opposite direction of her mother's yells.

"Girl, where you going? Lark? Get your narrow behind back here."

Lark ignored Honey, started running.

She had to get away.

Kenya's house.

That's where she'd go.

She ran for three blocks before her legs started to get weary. Panting, lungs burning, she slowed from a full-out trot to a leisurely walk. The image of the man and woman in the Lincoln was burned into her brain. It had horrified her. But it had excited her, too. That was hard to admit, but true just the same. All kinds of thoughts swirled in her mind. Kenya was her best friend, no doubt. And she was worried about her girl, true. But. But. But. The Lincoln episode, as she was now calling it, had stirred something in her she couldn't deny. Passion. Desire. Want. Donovan had fumbled with her bra straps more times than she could count. Fumbled over his words every time she covered his hands with her own and let him know things had gone as far as she would allow them to. Maybe it was time to move beyond the fumbling. Maybe it was time to seal the deal. She felt something, right down between her legs in that naughty place, that she couldn't pretend away.

Kenya was her best friend, no doubt.

And she was worried about her girl, true.

But.

She was growing up, getting ready to leave for college. Having these feelings. These desires. These wants. The man and woman in the Lincoln had just reminded her of what she already knew, of what she was already aware. She wanted to feel a man, experience a man, the way a woman did. There it was.

Donovan was away.

But there were more than a few boys that had been sniffing after her that weren't away.

Some of them lived in the vicinity.

She contemplated making that bad move.

But God works in mysterious ways.

The loud honk of a horn startled her. A dusty Jeep Wrangler, looked like it hadn't been washed since it was driven off the lot, had moved up next to her at the curb. She glanced at it, then looked straight ahead, kept moving. The sky was black, the street covered in shadows. Another light tap sounded on the horn. That time she didn't glance in the Jeep's direction. Picked up the pace of her walk.

"Hey."

She picked up the pace some more. Not quite a run, but more than a walk.

"Hey" again.

She didn't have Mace. Did have her house keys, though. Gouge an eye with the sharp, jagged keyhole end if need be.

"Don't be alarmed. Cool ya heels a moment."

Something in the masculine voice caught her attention. Something familiar. Lark knew better, but she still slowed. Looked over at the Jeep. Squinted her eyes. He'd brought the car to a complete stop, was leaning over, his head visible in the passenger-side window.

Lark should have been startled.

Red flags everywhere.

But she wasn't.

"Did you…did you…follow me?" she asked.

"No. No," he said then shook the blond dreads from his eyes so she could see the sudden sincerity in them. "Well, yeah, I guess. Yeah, I did."

"Why?" The only question that came to mind. Later, she'd think of so many other things she should have said. So many other things she should have done.

"How old are you?"

"Seventeen." In a few months.

He groaned. "You're beautiful. Never would have guessed it."

"Me?"

"Yes."

Something Lark didn't hear often. Even from Donovan. Despite the compliment, she managed to gather herself. "Why did you follow me?"

"I didn't. At first."

She just looked at him.

"Look, my name's Trent."

"Lark."

"Beautiful name, Lark."

"Uh-huh. Why did you follow me?"

He sighed. "I got off shift after you and your folks left. Saw you all in the parking lot, twenty minutes after I'd cleared your table, trying to get your father in the car."

Lark closed her eyes briefly, relived that nightmare.

"I shouldn't have followed," Trent said. "I know better. But something about you…"

Lark heard it then. In his voice. Unmistakable. Lust. Highly inappropriate, she knew. "How old are you, Trent?"

"Closer to forty than twenty."

Lark came to her senses. Remembered Kenya's drama last year. Her friend's thin escape. The tragedy that could have happened because Kenya got in a car she shouldn't have. Kenya was her friend, no doubt. With her always, even now. So many unreturned text messages. Lark was worried, had to get over there. The feelings the Lincoln episode had stirred in her, gone. The older blond dread, as sexy and intriguing as he was, just couldn't happen.

"I've g-gotta go," she stammered and started moving.

"Wait, wait."

She didn't. Let her legs move her up the block, where she hid in the cover of shadow.

He didn't press. Thank God. Didn't follow.

Only a couple blocks from Kenya's, her heartbeat settled and she started to feel better. Some sisterhood laughter with her best friend was all the medicine she needed. On Kenya's block her pace picked up. She couldn't wait to tell Kenya about everything.

And then...

A sight she was familiar with around her way, around the projects. But Kenya's neighborhood was quiet, uneventful, calm. Usually. The hood still, but a gentler variety of hood.

A sight that didn't cause Lark any pause at her project housing.

The flashing strobe of a police car.

In front of Kenya's house.

And the sound of Kenya's mom, wailing.

chapter 13

Eric

I needed a Coke bottle cap of air. That's all. I stepped outside of Benny's house to get it, and left him in the den with Endia and Tanya. My nerves were jangled. Something inside of me didn't feel quite right. A good day, what should have been one of my best ever, was shaping up otherwise. In the cool of the evening, I thought about my sister. There were tears in her eyes—such an unusual and unexpected memory. I thought about Fiasco, too. He was out on the road, alone, struggling with the one thing that had always been his refuge, struggling with his music. Lately he'd begun to question his relevance in the ever-changing taste of hip-hop music fans. I'd let Kenya and Fiasco down that day, and I couldn't elbow my guilt out of the way. The guilt bullied me. It pressed up against me, chest to chest.

It was winning.

"I did something wrong."

It wasn't a question. Endia's voice was so soft it startled me. It was filled with sadness, too. In Mama's darker moments she always talked about the burden women carried on their shoulders. She said women spent the better parts of their lives apologizing to men.

I wanted no part of that.

Living in a house of women had made me sensitive to their emotions.

"No," I told Endia. "You didn't do anything wrong."

She smiled, moved farther into the garden.

The area where I stood was centered with a coral fountain, a patio of rust-colored stones beneath my feet. Greenery everywhere. I didn't know what the stuff was, didn't watch enough Discovery Channel to be knowledgeable about it, but I gave everything names. Bougainvillea, roses, the erect stems of patchouli bushes. A strong whiff of peat was in the air, mulch spread everywhere.

"Can I stand with you?" Endia asked.

I hesitated long enough to turn her eyes even sadder. "Please, E?" she said.

"You don't have to call me that. Eric's fine."

"Eric." She pursed her lips, made her way over to me, took my hand. I resisted a little bit at first, but in a matter of seconds we were holding hands like longtime lovers. The sky was dark and filled with stars. A romantic night. Suddenly my nerves were rattled for a third reason other than Kenya and Fiasco. Endia. She was starting to feel like a girl-friend to me. I'd never had one. Didn't know how that went.

But I wanted one.

I wanted her.

"Going back to school in a few weeks," I said. "I'm one of if not the most popular boys in my school."

"I bet." Endia squeezed my hand, then laid her head on my shoulder.

Crickets chirped. Mosquitoes buzzed by. Lightning bugs lit the darkness. A cool breeze blew. I kept my eyes on the stars. "Up until almost the end of the year, last year, I was the exact opposite," I said. "I was as unpopular as a person could be. The butt of all the jokes. Didn't fit in with the dudes. The girls only dealt with me if it was to their benefit. I tutored more stupid girls than any man should ever have to in one lifetime."

Endia chuckled.

"My nickname was Poser, a play on my last name. Not a good one, either, as you can see. I can't tell you how many days I came home, locked myself in my room and cried. Or how many nights I prayed to God to either make me popular or take me away."

I'd never told anyone that.

Other than Mya, I didn't share my private pain, my personal humiliation, with anyone. I smiled through the insults. Kept my head high. Walked around as if it all just rolled off of my back.

But it didn't.

It hurt.

Hurt more than words could ever convey.

Endia was silent, her head still on my shoulder. I peeked at her, saw her watching the stars, too. I went on. "You'd never know it if you judged my popularity by the number of MySpace friends I have. Or the number of dudes that will rush to give me dap the first day back. Or the girls that will giggle and whisper when I come around. But that's all fake. I only got popular because I met Fiasco."

I'd spent months reveling in my newfound popularity. Walking around with my chest out. Swagger came naturally to me all of a sudden, just as it did with all the other cool boys. I didn't have to practice my walk in front of my mirror anymore. I didn't have to obsess over what I wore. My natural walk was as smooth as a Robin Thicke ballad, and whatever I rocked immediately became hot. Instead of following trends, I set them. Instead of copying the cool boys, I showed them how to move through life with swag.

But it was all a lie.

And suddenly I felt exposed.

Naked.

Shed from that protective skin.

I wasn't E. I was Poser. Poser, Poser, Poser.

"You done?" Endia said.

I nodded.

"Can we sit in the gazebo, Eric?"

I nodded. She led the way. Fingertips to fingertips, she pulled me into the gazebo. It was bananas. Strong wood. An architectural marvel with grooved spindles and Victorian-style corner braces. And a swing.

We sat on the swing.

I stopped looking at the stars.

Looked at Endia's eyes instead.

For me, it was one and the same.

"I did a Google search on your name," Endia said. "Looked for you on MySpace. Couldn't find anything."

"Should've just asked."

She shook her head. "You don't understand. I mean last year, after I met you in the mall."

"What? Get out of here."

"I did, Eric."

"Why would you do that? I was such a lame when I met you."

"I didn't think you were so lame."

I looked at her, hard. Searched for the truth. She held my gaze. It didn't look like she was lying.

"Why?" I whispered.

"You don't know how wonderful you are?"

If I could have spoken I would have. But I couldn't. I shook my head. I didn't know how wonderful I was. Because I wasn't wonderful. Not even close.

"You were so easy to talk to," Endia said. "And you weren't all up on me like most of these boys. You were funny. Smart." She paused, smiled. "Cute in a cornball way."

"Thanks," I said.

She playfully tapped my shoulder. "No. I really thought you were cute."

"I've thought about you every day since I met you," I said. "Went over everything I did wrong a million times. Dreamed about getting another shot with you."

"And I stalked you on the Internet," she said.

I laughed. "I met Fiasco that same day I met you. Did I ever tell you that?"

"No. Serious?"

"Yup. In that same store at the mall. He saw me with you. He schooled me on all I did wrong."

"You didn't do anything wrong, Eric."

I narrowed my eyes. "You gave me your phone, and I was too stupid to save my number in it."

Endia nodded. "There was that...."

"I felt so badly after we met," I said. "Felt like I really needed to do something to redeem myself. Vote, pray, donate some clothes to the Red Cross."

Endia laughed. "See what I'm talking about? You're funny."

Silence settled between us.

I didn't have anything else to say.

I was content just sitting there with her.

"Went to a party last year," Endia said after a while. "Mostly older kids but they let me and Tanya in. They were drinking. Smoking. Tanya wasn't comfortable. She wanted to leave almost as soon as we got there. I was cool, though. I told her to go, that I was staying. And she did. She left. When she walked out, they were all calling her weak. I joined in that chorus. But really I was the weak one."

I listened.

"I smoked weed for the first and last time that night, Eric. Had some drinks. This boy, Michael, offered to take me home. I went with him. He tried to get at me, but thankfully I was clearheaded enough to dead that. And he didn't stress me, either. I was grateful for that. Until the next day." Endia's voice softened even more than usual. "All day I heard lies about what I'd done with Michael. He wouldn't set 'em straight, either. Tanya wasn't there, so she didn't defend me.

To this day I think she thinks it was all true. I had to change my MySpace page to private because of all the hateful, rude comments I was getting."

"I'm sorry," I said.

She nodded. "Thought all kinds of crazy stuff about not wanting to be here." Tears. It was that kind of day, I guessed. I rubbed her shoulders for comfort.

"I heard that J. Holiday song on the radio," she said. "'Bed.' And I thought it was such a beautiful song. He was talking about taking the girl to bed, but it was still nice. How I'd want it to be. Respectful, special, not after a night of smoking weed and drinking. You know?" She looked at me, so I nodded. "I didn't know the title or the artist," she continued. "I caught the end of the song on the radio. So I went to the mall to try and find it." She wiped her eyes, halted the tears. "And there you were."

"There I was."

"If you remember, Eric, I was alone."

"Ditto," I said.

She squeezed my hand. "We all have our problems. Part of growing up, I suppose. And then when you do grow up, you'll have different problems."

"True."

"I lied to you the other day at the diner, Eric."

I knew this sunshine was really a cloud without a silver lining. I swallowed, steadied myself. If I were in a car I would've strapped on my seat belt at that point. I just knew a collision was about to happen. "Tell me."

"I knew who you were the second you walked up to our table. And I didn't forget that J. Holiday song. Believe me. I was stunned to see you. So nervous about seeing you again. And you remembered me. That blew me away. Such a surprise."

I sighed, undid my imagined seat belt.

"Can I be bold?" I said.

"Yeah."

Her lack of hesitancy gave me courage. I took a deep breath. "Will you be my—?"

"Yes," Endia cut me off.

"I didn't even finish."

"Whatever you want me to be, Eric. I want to be it."

Wow!

"My girlfriend?"

"Yes."

My smile was the widest this world has ever known. My heart punched my chest. I had a girlfriend. And it was Endia. All the times I'd scribbled her name on notepads must have paid off for me.

"This is unbelievable," I said.

"Truly."

All of my woe-is-me thoughts were gone. Just like that. Maybe I was wonderful after all. Maybe the swagger I thought was fake had always been with me. Fiasco had just helped me refine it. Endia did say she was feeling me. And that was before Fiasco's counsel. Maybe the kids accepted me now for me, and not just because I was friends with Fiasco. That friendship just made them take their blinders off, give me a chance, and now they realized what Endia said she knew from gate. I was a wonderful dude.

"Can I be bold, Eric?" Endia asked.

"Yeah."

She reached over, took my face in her hands, framed it with her warm touch. Leaned in. Kissed me. I was lost in her warmth, with my eyes closed. We stayed like that for minutes. It was beyond anything I'd ever experienced before. We would have probably stayed like that for the rest of the evening.

But Benny's voice broke us apart.

Busted.

He was standing by the edge of the garden. His pale white skin was chalkier than ever. Endia leaned away from me, fixed her clothes. I cleared my throat. "You didn't answer your phone, E," Benny said. "You didn't hear it ringing?"

"On vibrate," I said and patted my pocket. It wasn't there. I stood up, saw it had fallen out. It rested against the cushion of the swing. I picked it up.

Six missed calls.

Dayum.

I was about to check and see who was blowing me up.

"Your mom called the house, E," Benny said.

I said the typical thing, expecting the typical answer. "Everything okay?"

Benny shook his head. "Kenya."

chapter 14

Kenya

> *I must tell Je-sus all of my trials*
> *I can-not bear these burdens alone*
> *In my dis-tress He kindly will help me*
> *He ev-er loves me and cares for His own*
> *I must tell Je-sus, I must tell Je-sus*

the soft, red cushioning of the church pews absorbs the melodic voices of the choir, absorbs the wails of the mourners, absorbs the anguished heat coming off of those mourner's bodies. Funerals always seem to be hot. It's a heat that even air-conditioning can't chase away. Flower arrangements are everywhere. The church is packed. I walk down the center aisle, toward the mother-of-pearl casket situated just below the pulpit in the middle of the church. I notice a few students from high school—girls I swore were jealous of me, dudes that tried to kick it to me constantly. I speak to 'em as I move past. They look right through me. Look right past me.

Pastor Hubbs is in the pulpit, dressed in a regal black robe. Beads of sweat cover his forehead. He sweats a lot. He taps the microphone, clears his throat. His deep baritone fills the church. It commands attention. Not another sound can be heard. "It is with the greatest sympathy," he says, "that I come before you, celebrating the life of one who left us too soon but now lies at peace in the arms of He that made us."

A few murmurs of amen.

I continue walking down the center aisle, unashamed that I'm the only one besides Pastor Hubbs on my feet.

"The past week has been a time of great reflection. Reflection on the life of this precious soul. Brothers and sisters, I've run different words through my mind in preparation of this moment. How to confront the loss of one so young, so precious, with so much more to accomplish. What words to say that might be of comfort to this grieved mother, this grieved brother, words that might help them to carry on." Pastor Hubbs's gaze is fixed on me as I walk toward him. His arms are outstretched as if beckoning me to come to him.

I'm coming.

"I wish I had some magic words of comfort. Unfortunately, I do not. It will take every ounce of my faith, and yours, to endure this loss. My message to you: Hold to His hand. In this dark hour. Hold to His hand. In the darker hours to come. Hold to His hand. Faith must be both our bridge and shelter." He stops, wipes the bucket of sweat off his brow with a white-as-snow handkerchief he keeps balled in his fist throughout his sermons. "Oh," he sings, "we must try not to question this. Not my will, but Thine will be done."

I'm twenty paces from the casket.

I'm close.

"Jesus is our strength and our redeemer."

Fifteen paces away.

"Our shelter in a time of storm."

Ten paces.

"The Alpha and Omega."

Five.

I pass by Mama on the first pew. Her eyes shine with tears.

Eric is at her left shoulder, dressed in black, handsome as ever, but stricken, too. Looks like some illness has gripped him and won't let go. His skin is lacking color, his shoulders are lacking strength, he looks skinnier than I ever remembered him.

I'm in a blue dress. Hair done up. More makeup than usual. Teardrop earrings. My grandmother's antique broach around my slim neck. Mama always promised me that passed-down bling for the day when I got married.

I look good.

Always.

But I look especially good today.

"We must celebrate her ascension to her eternal rest," Pastor Hubbs says. "God in His infinite wisdom has called her home."

Tears find my eyes as I look into the casket.

It's like looking in a mirror.

I look good, my eyes closed, hands clasped over my chest.

Peaceful.

At rest.

Mama's in the living room of our place. There are people everywhere. The house carries some good smells. Food mostly. Fried chicken. Collard greens. Apple and coconut pie.

"Can I do anything for you?" someone asks Mama.

Mama looks up. Her eyes are dead. "Make it '73 again. Put on the O'Jay's "Love Train." Or pop in a movie. Al Pacino. *Serpico.* I want to return to that happy time, before I lost my child, my baby girl. Can you do that? Can you do that?"

No one answers.

Mama's voice raises a notch. "Can you do that?"

Again, no one answers.

Mama dissolves into tears.

I hate to see her cry.

I rush out of there, head past everyone, move out into our backyard.

Standing against the fence that faces our neighbor, his back to me, is Donnell.

By himself, a red plastic cup in his hand.

"Why are you out here by yourself?" I ask.

Donnell turns sharply, taken surprise by my voice from over his shoulder, I guess.

"You're messing this up, Kenya," he says.

"What I do?"

"I'm not supposed to see you."

"Just wanted to talk to you."

He sighs. "You could have used the phone. You know I'm not supposed to see you."

"I'm contrarian. You know that."

He frowns. "You're what?"

"Contrarian."

He shakes his head, smiles. "College did you some good."

"No doubt. The best years of my life."

"A Delta is what an Ah-ka ain't..." he chants, surprising me.

He has an accomplished look on his face, his arms up. I walk to him, straighten the collar on his tuxedo, fall into his embrace. It's so comfortable in his arms.

"Boris Kodjoe and Taye Diggs ain't got nothing on you," I say.

He lifts my veil, leans down, kisses me. His lips are full, warm, sensual. Hardly anything in this world can compete with a kiss from Donnell. We kiss for a few minutes. Then, suddenly, I pull away, shoo him off of me like he's a pesky fly. "You're gonna ruin my makeup, boy. I want this day to be perfect."

"Planned for it like Star Jones."

"It has to be perfect," I say.

"Close your eyes, Kenya," Donnell says. "And when you open them, you'll be my wife."

I close my eyes.

* * *

I open my eyes.

Donnell's nowhere in sight. Neither is my backyard. I'm in strange surroundings, lying in a bed not my own, covered with a thin white blanket that is as coarse as sandpaper. A soft light is over my head. The smell of Bengay hits my nose. Or is that alcohol? My head is throbbing, mouth is dry and my body aches. A small table on wheels is next to my bed. On it is a pitcher of water, what looks like a television remote, some papers and a bouquet of flowers.

Pieces of understanding come to me.

Slowly.

But it comes just the same.

I was in an accident.

"You're awake. Good timing."

The origin of the voice is a thin, freckled woman with reddish hair. She has the greenest eyes I've ever seen. Despite being thin, her face is full; she has chipmunk cheeks. She's wearing a white lab coat over a flowery top, has a clipboard in her hands. Short nails on her fingers, no nail polish. She looks like a woman who'd wear nail polish. Something in a plum color.

"I was at my funeral...then I was getting married," I manage to say.

She nods. "Dreaming, Kenya. We've given you some pretty strong medicine."

"I'm in the hospital."

"You are. I'm Dr. Burress. Does your head hurt, Kenya?"

Right to the questions.

"No," I say.

"Vision at all blurred?"

"No."

She scribbles something on her clipboard.

"What happened to me?" I ask. "Am I okay?"

"An accident," she says. "You don't remember?"

"Li'l bit." I look down at my legs, afraid to try and wiggle my toes, afraid I won't be able to. "Am I okay?"

"Don't think you have a concussion."

But I'm in the hospital. My own bed.

"What *do* I have?"

Dr. Burress moves closer to the bed, pours me a cup of water. "Bet your mouth is dry." She moves the cup by my lips. I lean forward as much as I can, gulp it down in one big swallow.

"You broke a few ribs," she says. "We have you immobilized."

Touches my stomach.

I notice the vestlike thing wrapped around me for the first time.

She goes on. "Lacerated liver."

"That...?" I can't form the words.

I want to know if I'm going to die.

"I know it all sounds scary, Kenya. But you're in good hands. This is one of the best trauma hospitals in the country. You'll be fine."

Trauma?

"Why am I here?"

She clears her throat, places her clipboard on the table, next to the water pitcher. I could use another drink of water, but I don't ask.

"You have a pneumothorax, Kenya."

"English?"

"A collapsed lung. There are two types. Tension, which is a total collapse of one or both lungs. And simple, which is a partial collapse."

The dread in her voice lets me know that neither is a walk in the park.

"We've done chest X-rays. Thankfully, yours is simple. Not to minimize it, because you'll have some challenges ahead of you."

Challenges?

"You'll probably have sharp, stabbing chest pain with your breathing from time to time. That's known as a pleuritic state. Pain in your shoulders or back is also common. A dry, hacking cough."

"I'm gonna live?"

She smiles. "Yes. Absolutely."

"I'm going away to college in a couple of weeks."

"Kenya…"

"No." I shake my head. "Please don't tell me…"

"Kenya…"

"How long will I be here?" I ask.

"That I can't say at the moment," she says. "We'll monitor you. Once we have the lung under control, we'll remove your chest tube, and, barring infection, you should be close to release at that point."

Her words come at me seemingly a million miles per hour. But I'm sharp. I catch most things. "Chest tube?"

She touches my right arm. Rolls the sleeve of my hospital gown up to my shoulder. My eyes start to tear up at the sight.

She pats me calmly. "We put a small incision under your armpit to feed in the tube. You're gonna be fine."

A million thoughts run through my head.

I speak only one.

"Where's my family, Dr. Burress?"

chapter 15

Eric

WE were all together in the hospital waiting room for family and friends of the patients. Mama and Hollywood were seated next to one another. Hollywood was quieter than usual, rubbing Mama's shoulder, occasionally whispering in her ear. All the negative thoughts I had regarding him disappeared. I'd never look down my nose at him again. He was calm, caring, everything I ever hoped for in a man for my mama. Everything I hoped for in a father for myself. Sometimes it takes tragedy to bring out the best in people. When Hollywood spotted me watching him, he nodded, pursed his lips in a smile. I nodded in return. But I didn't smile.

Mama had finally stopped crying. She sat in a daze, though. I'm not sure she was even aware of anyone in the room besides Hollywood. And that's only because he was so close to her, was in physical contact. He couldn't be denied.

I couldn't sit myself. I'd burned a hole in the carpet, walked from one end of the room to the next. I was glad no one had told me to sit down. I was glad for a lot.

Lark, Kenya's best friend in this entire world, had a *People* magazine in her lap. It was open to a story about Janet Jackson's weight loss, but Lark hadn't read a single word. She kept glancing down at the page, then looking away. She bounced her knee nervously. Her nerves made my nerves even worse than they were.

Endia had sent me a text message: Thinking of you.

Benny had, too: I prayed for her, E.

Endia's text was chicken soup for my soul.

I had someone in my corner.

Benny's text almost made my eyes water.

I'd prayed for her, too.

Begged God, and made Him promises I was prepared to keep.

Lark's leg stopped bouncing. She sat bolt upright in her chair, and her eyes fixed on something across the room.

I turned.

A green-eyed white woman, with freckled skin and reddish hair, wearing the warmest of smiles, was standing in the doorway of the waiting room.

"She's awake," she said. "She wants to see you all."

No one moved.

Then someone did.

Hollywood.

He stood up, took Mama's hand, then turned to me and Lark, offered us an outstretched hand.

The three of us let him guide us to Kenya's room.

All of us paused at the threshold, even Hollywood.

We weren't sure what awaited us inside.

I prayed yet again.

Swollen.

Kenya's beautiful face was so swollen. Her eyes were tight; it was obvious she was in incredible pain. Wires and tubes were everywhere. I noticed one tube in particular. It was fed from her armpit. Mama took the hardest breath I'd ever heard. Lark started to cry. Hollywood stood over Kenya's bed, breathing heavily himself. I stood off in the distance, my emotions in check.

"Come give your sister some love, Eric," Kenya said.

Her mouth was swollen like everything else.

Words came out muffled. Her words were understandable, but muffled.

I moved to the bed. My lip trembled. I had a hard time catching my breath.

I didn't want Kenya to notice.

Of course, she did.

"Breathe, dawg, breathe," she said.

Dialogue from *Training Day*. A Denzel Washington movie. We'd watched it together.

I smiled.

"I know," Kenya said.

"I'm sorry. I'm sorry."

"Don't say that. You didn't do anything."

She was right. I hadn't done anything. That was the problem.

"All right, no more crying up in here. Everybody get yourselves together."

Mama.

There was a sudden strength to her voice.

I wiped my eyes. My fingers came back wet. I hadn't even known I'd shed tears.

Lark did, too.

Hollywood cleared something from his throat.

"God is good," Mama said. "And this family is strong." Hollywood's hand hadn't left from around her waist since we'd entered the room. "We're gonna get through this."

"I didn't do this to get out of driving Eric around, I swear," Kenya said.

More tears.

Laughter.

We would get through this.

A woman in tan khaki pants and a sophisticated white blouse came in sometime later, interrupted us, asked Mama to step outside with her into the hall. Mama followed her outside. I looked at Hollywood. Lines were formed in his forehead, and his eyes followed Mama's every move. I recognized that look in his eyes. Love.

Mama wasn't outside in the hall for long. She came back in the room, an angry set to her jaw.

"Everything okay, Mama?"

"The Devil is a liar."

"What?"

"Nothing?" She waved it off.

Later, I'd find out the woman who'd pulled Mama outside was with hospital administration. Apparently, Mama's insurance was somewhat lacking.

My sister's care would pose a financial strain.

I was assigned a very uncomfortable task.

I was down in the hospital lobby, exchanging text messages with Benny and Endia, while I waited.

I saw him as soon as he pulled up.

I took a deep breath as I watched him rushing toward the hospital's entrance.

He came in the door like a gust of wind, saw me and almost crumpled.

"Eric?"

"She's okay."

His shoulders eased. "I got here as soon as I could. Thanks for calling me, man."

"No problem, Donnell."

I hated this.

"So she's okay?"

"Broken ribs, lacerated liver, collapsed lung." Recited what the doctor had recited to us.

Donnell frowned. "That's okay?"

"She's gonna live," I said.

He nodded. "Let's get up there."

I hated this.

He made a move. I didn't.

He saw I hadn't moved. "Eric?"

"Don't even know how to tell you this."

That's all I said.

He narrowed his eyes. Stood silent. "She doesn't want to see me?"

I shook my head. "No. She doesn't."

chapter 16

CSI was on. Lark couldn't care less. She wasn't the least bit interested. Her television had been dark for days, and she'd turned it on now just to break the monotony of silence in her bedroom. She liked it better silent, so she clicked the television back off. Donovan was still in Jamaica with his parents. They'd spoken a few times, but with each call she felt further and further away from him. He'd tried her today; she hadn't picked up.

She just wanted to stay in her room by herself.

No television, phone calls, music, food, showers.

Was she depressed?

Lark figured she had to be.

But who could blame her? Her best friend was…was…not herself. Lark couldn't think of Kenya as damaged, hurt, wounded or injured. None of those words. Kenya just wasn't her usual self. Yeah. That sounded all right. Felt okay.

Sleep.

That's what Lark needed. She'd been getting plenty of it, but no matter how many hours she kept her eyes closed, it wasn't enough. She'd wake up from a five-hour nap and find herself yawning within five minutes. Right back to sleep.

Sweet dreams.

At least she'd try for that.

She closed her eyes.

Prayed.

Asked God to make all the pain go away, if just for a little while. Asked Him to make her dream. Sweet dreams. God could be the director, like Spike Lee. She wanted to dream about the Delta party at school. Kenya blowing everybody away with her voice, her performance with Carolina and Tammy. That fine dude, JaMarcus, practically tripping over himself to get up in Kenya's space.

The girls looking so fly in cream and crimson.

A Delta is what an Ah-ka ain't, what a...

"You sleep?"

Lark's eyes shot open. She squinted against the light that rushed in the room from the hall. Anger bubbled up inside of her. She was a finger's width from having a sweet dream about Kenya. So close. And her mother ruined it. Typical. Lark felt like running away. Hitting something. Hitting someone.

Honey.

Her mother stepped in the room, left the door open behind her, let in light.

"Brought you some..."

Honey stopped in her tracks, set the plate of food she'd prepared on Lark's dresser, moved to the wall, hit the light switch. More light invaded the room. Lark wanted it dark. Didn't want to see herself, or anyone else, clearly. But she didn't even bother to cover her eyes against the light. Didn't have the desire or the strength in her arms.

"Crying in the dark," Honey said.

"Wasn't crying, Mama."

"I know a li'l something about crying in the dark." Honey sighed, took a seat at the foot of Lark's bed.

Lark wanted to roll over, show Honey her back. She had the desire, but lacked the strength to do that one simple thing.

"I'm really sorry about your friend."

"Kenya. Her name's Kenya." Angry.

"Kenya. I'm sorry about Kenya."

"Don't worry about it."

Honey grunted, sat silent.

"Shut the door on your way out," Lark said. "Please."

Threw that *please* on at the end, as Honey would say.

Honey stood, moved over to the door, shut it.

To Lark's dismay, her mother shut herself in the room, hadn't left. "I don't feel like talking," Lark said.

"Listen, then."

Honey moved back to the bed, sat next to Lark instead of at the foot. Lark found the strength, rolled over, gave her back to Honey. Honey's voice was soft, insistent. Softer than Lark had ever remembered. She had to struggle to hear her mother. Not that she actually cared about what Honey had to say. It didn't matter.

"Never really had a friend like that. Like you and Kenya. Met your daddy when we were both so young. We're all each other has ever known. I'm his only real friend. He's mine."

"With friends like that..." Lark began.

"Who needs enemies," Honey finished. "You're upset. I'll humor you."

Lark wasn't gonna say it.

"We were good friends," Honey said. "Way back when."

"Before me," Lark said. It hurt to say it. But she knew it was true.

"You're right," Honey said.

Lark bit her lip. The conversation was done as far as she was concerned.

"You wondered if I was in college when I got pregnant with you?" Honey waited for Lark to respond. It didn't happen. "Well, I was. Rider University. Your dad was at Montclair State."

Her dad? In college? That was a revelation for Lark.

But she didn't dare respond.

This conversation was over.

"He had this beat-up Buick. I believe it was a Century. He'd come see me every weekend. Send me letters every day.

To this day, I don't know how he did it, but there'd be a letter in my box at school every day."

Her voice dripped honey.

Lark wasn't moved.

Her dad had gone from Hallmark to Hennessy.

"He wanted to work on Wall Street. A broker or something. I wanted to be a psychologist. I was always interested in how the mind works."

How different might life have been?

Maybe they'd have a house instead of living in the projects.

"Sorry I messed it all up for you guys," Lark said. "You both had to drop out and forego your dreams."

"Your dad didn't drop out."

"What?"

"He graduated."

"What? How? I mean…" Lark was beyond confused.

She couldn't help it. She turned over, faced her mother.

Honey's smile was sad and warm at the same time.

"He graduated. I dropped out to have you. We got married. He made me promise to go back once you hit school age."

"Daddy has a degree?"

Lark still couldn't wrap her mind around that.

Her father's best friend had been his hands for as long as she could remember. Construction, masonry, carpentry. She'd never seen him in a suit except for when Nana died. When Pop-Pop passed he'd worn slacks and a plaid shirt. She couldn't imagine him behind a desk, his fingers hovering over a keyboard.

"He tried for work. But he had a difficult time finding it in his field. So he just…worked. Did whatever he could to support us. At first he still looked. Then he gave up. Work was work. But I tell you, a part of your father died when he gave up."

"And you?" Lark asked.

"Work was work," Honey said.

"So you got stuck raising me and never went back to school?"

"I raised you."

Lark snorted. "I scarred you so badly you didn't even have any more kids. Not that I would suggest you did."

You weren't any good with the one you had.

A thought in Lark's head, left unspoken.

"Couldn't," Honey said. "Had complications with your birth."

"What?"

Honey smiled. Sad and warm. "I got my baby, but there'd be no others."

Lark thought, *What a sad and sorry life.*

"Life's gonna be sad at times," Honey said. "Don't feel sorry for me. That's not why I'm telling you all of this."

Oops. Had Lark spoken out loud?

"Why are you telling me all of this then, Mama?"

"Your father and I haven't dealt with the bumps in the road as well as I would've liked. You don't have to make the same mistake. I want you to go off to school and do all the great things I know you're capable of doing."

Lark hunched her eyes in surprise.

Honey was talking clearly, grammatically correct and with a warmth Lark had never known. Lark had thought her mother had interrupted her sleep, broke off her dream about Kenya. But that must not have happened. Obviously, she was dreaming now.

Lark pinched herself.

Damn!

Honey laughed. "You're awake, child."

Child. Not chile.

Damn!

"I don't understand," Lark said.

"I love you."

"What?"

"I love you."

"You've...you've never..."

"Told you that before? Yeah. Shame on me."

Tears.

Big, fat tears.

In Honey's eyes.

Honey sniffed. "When you love someone, you should do the best by them. I haven't, and I'm sorry for it. Your father hasn't. I won't even say we've tried. We've made so many mistakes." Honey reached forward, touched Lark's shoulder. "I'm proud of you for getting accepted to college. For figuring out how to pay for it on your own. Your father and I have a couple dollars saved up for you that we didn't tell you about."

"How much?" More and more revelations. Lark wasn't sure her heart was strong enough for all of this.

"You won't have to work. Except on your papers and classwork."

Tears.

Big, fat tears.

In Lark's eyes.

"Don't want to go...without Kenya," Lark said.

"Go in her honor."

It hit Lark immediately.

In Kenya's honor.

"That's a great idea, Lark."

"Yeah? You mean it?"

Carolina's voice was strong and excited through the phone line. "Yes. I mean it. The Deltas are a sisterhood of action. We were planning a concert anyway; always do to open the school year. We'll dedicate some of the proceeds to help Kenya's family with their medical bills. It'll be lovely, and for a good cause. We have to get her better, her bills paid, and here in school where she belongs. With her sisters."

"True dat." Lark felt her old self resurfacing.

She'd watch *CSI* today.

Eat, listen to some music, take a shower.

"I'll handle everything," Carolina said.

"Thank you so much."

"And you think you can get Fiasco to perform?"

"Spoke to Kenya's brother, and he talked to Fiasco. It's a go."

"That's great. I like his music."

"He's beefing with Yung Chit now. That should be interesting, them on the same stage."

"Not at the same time," Carolina said. "We'll keep that from happening."

"Be like a Delta and an Ah-ka sharing makeup."

Carolina growled like a cat.

They both laughed.

"So how's our girl doing?" Carolina asked.

"Better," Lark said.

Both Kenya and herself.

chapter 17

Kenya

"A benefit concert?"

"Yup."

"Whose idea is this?"

"Mine, Ken," Lark says. "You don't like it?"

"I'm a megalomaniac," I say. "'Course I like it."

Lark laughs. "You've been reading the dictionary Fiasco left you, huh, Ken?"

"One of the aides sits with me, reads it. I'm not quite strong enough to hold the book."

"What's his name?" Lark asks without missing a beat.

"Why it got to be a he?"

"What's his name, Ken?"

"I hate you."

"You love me, Ken. What's his name?"

"Terrence. You happy?"

"Black boy?"

"Yeah."

"Cute as *106 & Park* Terrence?"

"Cuter."

"Only you, Ken. Only you."

"I'm very sexy on a bedpan." I laugh.

Laugh to keep from crying.

Lark's a friend.

Check that, my best friend.

She knows me inside and out.

"You holding up okay, Ken?"

I bite my lip. "These four walls are driving me crazy. And I keep thinking about...school."

"JaMarcus?"

"Whatever, girl. I ain't thinking about that boy."

"You're better than me. Six-two—"

"Six-four," I cut in.

"Well, excuse me, Miss I-Ain't-Thinking-About-That-Boy."

Again, I laugh. Lark is medicine.

Better than Percoset, Vicodin, codeine.

I tell her so.

The accident has made me more willing to tell those I love that I love them.

"I love you, too, Ken," Lark says.

"Donnell's coming to see me today," I whisper.

Lark's eyes widen. "Shut up!"

I nod. "Yup."

"You finally approved his visit?"

"Yes."

"I need to go. Don't want you to see me boo-hooing."

"Yeah, you should go."

"You kicking me out, Ken?"

"Yes, ma'am. Don't want you to see me boo-hooing, either."

"Kenya?"

I open my eyes.

Dayum!

I fell asleep after Lark's visit. Didn't mean to do that, but these medicines are kicking my ass. Now I'm upset at myself. I didn't get a chance to prepare.

"Donnell," I say.

"How are you feeling?"

"I've had better days."

He nods, frowns.

"How is your mother?" I ask.

"Doing well. Taking therapy. Speech, physical, occupational. I was joking with her yesterday, told her she spent so much time down in the rehab's gym she was gonna come out looking like Nelly."

"50 Cent," I say.

"Reggie Bush."

"Flo Rida."

Donnell purses his lips. "How you get me talking about all these buff dudes?"

Buff?

Donnell's got the soul of a forty-year-old, I swear.

I love that about him, though.

He's solid.

"Speaking of buff," I say, "you're looking pretty good yourself. Been working out?"

"I'm allergic to the gym."

"What about your push-ups, sit-ups, crunches?"

"Yeah. I still do 'em."

"Two hundred of each every day, right?"

"Most."

We'll do anything to avoid the real issue. Donnell's forehead is creased with lines. The flesh around his eyes is puffy. Eyes aren't quite as clear as usual. Lips look dry.

"For real, though," I say. "How have you been holding up?"

He shrugs as an answer.

"I'm sorry I've kept you from seeing me."

He nods. "I've been worried about you. Eric's kept me up to speed."

"I'm sorry."

"It's cool."

He says cool the way I spell it in my text messages.

Kewl.

"How did we get here?" I ask. It isn't the first time I've asked this question.

"I don't know, Kenya. But I don't like it." He sighs, places a vase of flowers I hadn't seen in his hands on the desk next to my bed. I've gotten flowers from so many people. But these mean the most to me. Even more than the arrangement my mother brought me.

"Ooh. You got me flowers."

Modest, he doesn't respond.

"What are they?"

"What?"

"The flowers. They're beautiful. What are they?"

He flips up a card at the edge of the bouquet. "Fields of Europe. Lilies, daisy poms, button poms, waxflower and salal." He looks up at me. A tight smile on his face.

"They're very thoughtful."

"That they are."

"Your mother really is doing okay?"

"It's a process. She's doing fine, Kenya."

"I miss you calling me YaYa."

"That so, Kenya?"

I want to ask him again how we got here.

"You ready for school?" I ask instead.

"Not much for me to do. I'm staying here, commuting."

"Don't know how long I'm gonna be in here."

"Yeah."

"I was accepted at Rutgers, too," I say.

Feeling him out.

"I've been doing a lot of thinking," I say.

"Have you?"

I smile. Mine is tight like Donnell's. "There's nothing much else to do in here."

"You can smell your flowers."

"What's that?"

"Nothing, Kenya."

I bat my eyes. "Can't I get one YaYa from you?"

"I don't think so, Kenya."

There's an edge to his voice I can't figure out.

I don't want to figure it out, either.

"I'm tired of water. Can you get me a soda?"

"Where from?"

"Vending machine at the end of the hall, I believe."

"Do anything to get me to spend money on you, huh, Kenya?"

I smile. "Just practice. Get used to it."

Instead of the return smile I expect, he swallows, digs in his pocket for change, then turns and leaves the room.

What's wrong?

Is he not getting my signals?

Why is this going so wrong?

Does he not understand that I'm trying to put the past behind us? That I'm looking forward, instead of over my shoulder? That Melyssa Bryan is in my rearview mirror?

"Sprite."

"I missed you." My voice is cheery, sweet.

"Wasn't gone but a minute," he says.

He won't play along. "Wipe the can off," I say. "Hold it up to my mouth."

He does, but his mouth is so tight. Deep lines form around his lips. So much for this gesture bringing us closer. I take a sip. "Thanks. Can you wipe my mouth?"

He does. With a napkin.

"Could have used your lips," I say.

"Don't know where they've been, Kenya."

"What?"

"Nothing."

"What crawled up your butt and died?"

He sighs, rubs his head, his eyes. "I'm tired, Kenya."

I will not be getting a YaYa.

"I know about tired. Pain, too."

"Maybe I shouldn't've come, Kenya."

"Must you keep calling me that?"

He knits his brows. "What? That's your name."

"Okay, Donnell. Don't say I didn't try."

"You have," he says. "I have. I guess it's just not meant to be."

I will not cry.

"You can go," I say.

"Okay."

"I really hate you right now, Donnell."

His face falls. For a second I think he's about to salvage this get-together. "I love you, Kenya," he says. "And always will. I hope you remember that."

That sounds so final.

So done.

So over.

"Thanks for the flowers," I say.

His eyes are ruined by the crease lines at their corners.

He nods, leaves without another word.

I snatch the card off of the flowers, ready to rip it up into the tiniest of pieces and rain them on the floor. But I stop. And everything comes into focus.

The flowers aren't from Donnell.

They're from JaMarcus.

With a message. *Waiting for you in Georgia, my peach.*

Dayum!

chapter 18

Fiasco

FIASCO bounced on his heels backstage, energized. He could feel the flow of blood in his veins. He hadn't felt this kind of energy in a while. It wasn't that large of a club, but it was packed. It was smoky like most of 'em: too dark, hot, the usual. But there was a certain kind of energy in the crowd tonight that hadn't been present in any of the other cities. Katrina had done some real damage to Louisiana, for sure, but the old girl still had some life in her legs. And so did Fiasco.

The DJ started cutting in with a KRS-One sample. "Let us skip back to what they called hip-hop."

Fiasco bounded from backstage, mic in his hand.

"How many of y'all love that real hip-hop?"

A roar from the crowd.

But not cheers.

Boos.

Fiasco worked through it. "They saying hip-hop is dead. Are we dead?"

Beer cups, some of them empty, some not, rained down on him.

Plus boos that were building in a crescendo, getting louder and louder.

"Hip-hop ain't dead. Close. But she's still breathing. Ain't that right."

The DJ was still cutting the KRS-One loop. "Let us skip back to what they called hip-hop."

It started so low Fiasco couldn't make it out at first. A low chant that built quickly, just as the boos from the crowd had. It was like a forest fire, roaring out of control in a matter of seconds.

Yung Chit, Yung Chit, Yung Chit.

Fiasco's show, drowned out with chants of his new nemesis's name.

"Holeup, y'all. Yo. Holeup."

He tried to stop the Yung Chit nonsense.

Yung Chit, Yung Chit, Yung Chit.

"Holeup. Yo. Holeup."

His mic was invisible and speechless. Like it wasn't even turned on.

Yung Chit, Yung Chit, Yung Chit.

He was in the Dirty South. Yung Chit country. Chit was religion down here. Chit was currency. Chit was health. Chit was everything that mattered.

Yung Chit was killing hip-hop. Killing it dead.

And Fiasco couldn't save hip-hop.

The chant grew louder and louder.

Fiasco didn't even get to perform one song. He gave up trying. Made a gesture to the crowd that would embarrass him later when it got played all over YouTube. Then he dropped the mic on the stage, didn't even place it back in the mic stand. Dropped it like a temperamental rock star throwing down a guitar. Straight up Mick Jaggered the mic. Stepped off the stage without having even really started his set.

Yung Chit, Yung Chit, Yung Chit.

"This is dangerous," Toya said.

"Feel free to keep it moving," Fiasco replied.

"Don't be hateful to me, please."

"Just saying I'd understand if you want to move on," Fiasco said. "Maybe Yung Chit has some room on his bus for you." He touched his temple, focused his eyes like he was really thinking. "Or does he even have a bus? Probably has a leisure jet."

He was upset, and Toya could understand. She wouldn't add to it, despite the fact he was talking to her like she was less than zero. "This is turning into something serious," she said.

They were back in the dressing room. Fiasco sipped a Vitamin Water, half listened to Toya. "Ain't nothing I can't handle," he said.

"This is getting dangerous. I'm scared."

"It ain't nothing," he repeated.

"This is Power 103, the home of hip-hop and R & B. I'm the voice of your choice, your girl Joosy. If you're just tuning in, I have Yung Chit on the line. Chit?"

"Yo, yo, yo."

"Before the break you said some tough things about your situation with Fiasco. We definitely don't want another Tupac versus Biggie situation. The community can't deal with that. You didn't mean that, did you?"

"Dude has disrespected me on several occasions, Joose. My fans go in. I gotta go in, too."

"I'm all for some healthy competition, Chit. Just keep it on wax. You've said some reckless things this afternoon. Can you guys keep it on wax?"

"Real n----- do real things."

"Fiasco's been quiet, Chit."

"He better be. He'll get rocked if he opens his mouth. Ever. I ain't playing wit' this."

"It's that serious, Chit?"

"It's that serious, Joose."

"Come on, Chit."

"I heard homeboy's down here in the Dirty touring. If he

*knows what I know, he'll get on that gay bus of his and head
back North. I got gunners everywhere. Ya heard?"*

"*Chit, come on. That's reckless talk.*"

"*This a reckless game, Joose.*"

"*Chit, come on.*"

"*I'm out, Joosy.*"

"*Chit... Hello, Chit. Damn. We'll be back y'all. Gotta pay
the bills.*"

Fiasco powered off the radio.

"Okay?" he said. "I heard it Tone."

He was back on the bus, headed to South Carolina. Toya
was asleep, finally. Just past two in the morning, Fiasco
couldn't shut his own eyes, restless. Tone apparently
couldn't, either. But then Tone never slept more than a couple
hours a night. He was a hustler, always on the grind. He'd
called Fiasco's cell just minutes before. "If you're on wheels,"
he'd said, "get to the radio and turn to Power 103. Now."

"I didn't like the tone of that, no pun intended," Tone said
now. "Sounds like this is getting serious."

"It's okay," Fiasco said.

"It might not be a bad idea to do like he said, come back
North. No need leaving yourself in harm's way down here."

Tone hadn't even heard about the fiasco at the club, no
pun intended, and Fiasco wasn't about to share.

"Got four more cities to do, Tone, and I'm doing them."

"You my dude. I don't want to have to bury you."

"I got this, Tone."

Tone sighed through the phone lines.

"Four more cities," Fiasco said. "Plus the benefit concert
at that college in Georgia." For Eric's big sister, Kenya.

"And Chit's gonna be there, too," Tone said.

Fiasco nodded, cracked his knuckles.

Yep. Chit was gonna be at the benefit concert, too.

Fiasco was looking forward to it.

"We outta here baby,
We outta here baby,
We outta here baby…"
Kanye West, "Barry Bonds"

chapter 19

Eric

"HOW much longer, Eric?"

I looked over my shoulder. Endia was moving around my room, picking things off my shelves, getting a handle on what made Eric the Great tick. Just a year ago I would've donated an organ to have a girl as beautiful as Endia in my room. Mama was at the hospital, would be leaving straight from there and going to work. Hollywood was working until late. I had the entire house to myself.

And Endia to myself, as well.

"Just a minute longer," I said. "Let me finish this post."

"Maybe I can help."

I shook my head. "You wouldn't find this interesting."

"Let me see."

She was at my side before I could object further. I had one of Benny's old laptops open on my desk. I was logged into my MySpace page. Writing a blog entry. I was going to publish the blog post as a bulletin for all of my MySpace friends to read, too. A double dose of hate spewed at my least favorite rapper.

"You don't like Yung Chit?" Endia asked.

"Can't say I'm a fan. No."

She wrinkled her nose in disgust, and then looked deeper at my screen. "Eric, what's an anathema?"

I didn't dare tell her.

I clicked the Submit button, sent my post into the cyber universe.

"You really don't like Yung Chit?"

"No."

"Why not?"

"He doesn't have any talent."

"I like him."

"I forgive you," I said.

She punched my shoulder.

"Let's do something," I said. "What do you want to do?"

It wasn't a loaded question, I swear.

But Endia got a look in her eyes that I recognized from late-night movies on HBO and Showtime. I had the run of the house. And she knew it. I thought about what that meant.

"What's up?" she asked.

"Thinking."

She pinched my cheek. "You're so cute when you're thinking."

"Oh, yeah?"

"Yup. I can always tell when you are, too. You get this intense look."

"And you like that?"

"Love it." Her voice was syrup.

She liked me thinking. It turned her on.

I started doing multiplications in my head.

Fractions.

The Periodic Table of Elements. *H* for Hydrogen.

Ran into some trouble as I tried to reconstruct Martin Luther King's "I have a Dream" speech. Judge me not by the number of friends I have on MySpace but by the content of the comments they leave on my page. Something like that.

"Eric, you hear me?"

"What?"

"I was talking to you."

Oops. Thinking too much, I guess.

"Sorry. What?"

"I figured out what we can do."

"What's that?" I said in my James Bond voice.

A wide smile covered her face. I stood up, looked down at her.

Might have even winked, I'm not sure.

She stood on her tiptoes, kissed me softly on the lips.

My insides rumbled like a subway.

"You had an idea of something we could do?" I asked.

"Yes." Her eyes widened.

"Yes," I said.

"I haven't even told you yet."

"Yes."

She gave me another kiss. "I think I have an idea of what it is," I said.

Her hand came out from behind her back. "Scatter-gories." she yelled.

"Then again, maybe I didn't," I said.

chapter 20

Kenya

I'm watching an infomercial on television for P90X. Rock-hard abs, lean muscle and the best body imaginable in just ninety days. I don't believe it, but I keep watching. This is pretty much all I can stomach watching. Used to be able to watch the judge shows: *Judy, Joe Brown, Mathis*. But I can't anymore. Too many of their cases involve auto-accident damages. I used to watch *CSI* on the low, though I'd never admit it to Lark. Not anymore. Too much of a risk of a car chase that ends badly. Can't do *Maury*. Too many broken relationships that are beyond repair.

So P90X.

"Bet that don't even work."

I've learned that life is full of surprises.

Nothing catches me off guard anymore.

But her appearance by my door is beyond anything I could've ever anticipated. I blink my eyes a few times to make sure they're focusing correctly. I open my eyes. She's still here. Standing in the doorway. She looks unsure. A first.

"You can come in," I say.

Don't ask why I do.

She steps into the room.

Skintight blue jeans, a cutoff T-shirt with Nasty Girl stenciled on the front, fake Steve Madden boots.

This girl is a one-trick pony.

"How are you, Kenya?"

"Oh, you do know my name?"

She nods.

"How did you get in here?" I ask.

She looks back over her shoulder, then returns her gaze to me, a sheepish smile on her face. "Wasn't nobody at the nurse's station. I kinda just walked on in."

"How did you know my room number?"

She shrugs, pops a bubble with her gum. "I've got some fam up in here. Work down in the kitchen."

I roll my eyes.

"I ain't come to give you no drama, Kenya."

"What did you come for?"

"Talk."

"Pull up a seat. Let's get to it."

I don't mean that literally.

But she moves to the corner of the room, grabs hold of the chair Hollywood usually sits in when he and Mama visit, slides the chair across the floor, parks it right next to my bed. She fingers the petals on some flowers in a colorful bouquet I have on my side table.

"Nice flowers," she says.

I swallow. "From a friend."

"They all that."

"What did you want, Melyssa?"

I don't have the patience to deal with her. But I'm curious.

"Female to female?"

"Sure. Whatever."

She went through the trouble of moving that chair by my bedside, but she doesn't sit in it. She hovers over me in a position that forces me to look her in the face. So many other things I'd rather do.

"I saw Donnell the other day," she says.

"And?" If they check my vitals anytime soon, my blood pressure will be off the charts, I'm sure.

"I said hi," she says. "And he answered back."

"What would you expect? You two were intimate."

Melyssa chuckles. "Gotta love how you talk, Kenya. But, nah, me and him just did it. You two were *intimate*."

"Why are you here?"

She looks away from me. "He spoke but wasn't any feeling in his voice. Donnell's a good dude, so he wasn't 'bout to straight diss me. But it ain't been a month since I laid down with him, and he don't feel nothing toward me."

I swallow. "You care about him?"

She looks at me. Hazel eyes. I'd never noticed that before. "Probably more than I put on. Yeah."

For some reason, that hurts.

"He's a free agent," I say. "Go for yours."

"You know that ain't possible, Kenya."

"And why not?"

"Donnell caught up already. And not with me."

I feel a lump in my throat, the rush of my quickening pulse in my ears. "Caught up?" I whisper. "With who?"

Melyssa snickers. "You serious?"

"With who?" I repeat.

"You, Kenya. Don't be stupid."

Me.

For a second, I feared the worse. Feared that he'd moved on and the whole world knew about it except for me.

"Me?" I say.

"You've got a real problem if you don't know how much Donnell loves you. Everybody knows it around the way."

"Loved," I say. "Past tense."

"Yeah, okay."

"You came here to stir up bad memories?" I ask.

"Nah. Just wanted to talk to you. I had a dream about

you. No homo. I just wanted to let you know something. Had to come tell you."

"I'm listening."

"You asked me..." She pauses. "That day."

Day of my accident.

"Yes?"

"You asked me that day if I wanted better for myself?"

"I remember."

"I ain't gonna get into all that," Melyssa says. "But I had that dream."

"So you came to tell me you weren't gonna answer a question you already didn't answer once?"

Melyssa laughs. "Hear me out."

"Go ahead."

She eyes me. Hazel eyes. "In my dream, I asked you the same thing you asked me."

"Did you?"

"We ain't ever gonna be friends, Kenya."

"That's a newsflash."

"But what you asked me was...was something a friend would ask."

"Oh, yeah?"

"And I feel bad you got hurt."

"That makes two of us," I say.

"So I had to return the favor. Had to come ask you that question."

"To ask me if I want better for myself?"

"Exactly."

"Injuries aside, I'm aiight, Melyssa."

"You think so, huh?"

I don't have an answer for the judgment in her voice.

chapter 21

Fiasco

"**You're** awake?"

"Yeah."

Toya moved outside, settled beside Fiasco. Her legs were bare, her top covered with one of Fiasco's shirts. She'd awakened from a pretty sound sleep, discovered the spot next to her in bed was empty and cool. He'd done what he'd done with her. But he hadn't slept with her afterward, really slept. He didn't cuddle with her, either.

"Couldn't get to sleep?" she asked.

"Didn't try." He brought the brown bag in his fist up to his lips, kissed the lip of the bottle inside the bag and swallowed some liquid happiness. It burned his throat but warmed his soul.

Toya nodded at the bottle. "What you got there?"

"Kool-Aid."

"Kool-Aid? Doesn't look like Kool-Aid."

Fiasco looked at her with hard, reddened eyes. "Yoon is dead and gone. I don't need this. Stay in your lane, Toya."

"Yoon?"

He took another sip, then nodded. "My mother."

"Oh." Toya looked off into the distance. It was a cool evening. The *M* and *O* on the motel sign weren't illuminated. Place still had vacancies. "HBO needs to be free. This place is a dump."

Fiasco leaned against the bus. They'd had engine problems, another inconvenience. The bus had just gotten repaired and returned to Fiasco that evening. In the meantime, he'd holed up with Toya in the motel. A dump, for sure.

Fiasco was wearing shorts and a wifebeater, his usual of late, no socks or shoes on.

"You should be careful, don't step on any glass," Toya said. "Broken bottles all over the place."

Fiasco eyed her, said nothing.

"Yoon? What is that?" Toya asked.

"Told you that was my mother."

"You know what I meant. What was she?"

"Toya? What are you?" Fiasco felt like being difficult.

"My family is from Barbados."

Fiasco softened some. She wasn't a bad woman.

"Korean," he said.

"Father's black, I take it?"

"Was."

"Sorry to hear dat."

Fiasco shrugged. "I was young. I ain't miss a beat."

"Oh, no?"

"Nope."

"Why are you so angry, Fiasco?"

"Ruben."

"What?"

"My name. Ruben. How come you've never asked?"

Toya smiled. The sadness in her eyes betrayed the smile. "Would you have told me?"

"Probably not," Fiasco admitted.

Toya blinked. And blinked some more. "South Carolina is nice."

"Think so?"

"Yeah. This is the farthest south I've ever been."

"Farthest you're going for now."

"What?"

"There's a Hilton. I'll put you up there."

"What about Georgia?"

Fiasco swallowed. "Nah. I don't want anybody with me in Georgia."

Toya didn't argue.

Wasn't any use.

chapter 22

Lark

Lark sat down at her desk and compiled a list of items
she'd need for college:

Alarm clock
Small storage trunk
Extralong twin sheets (80")
Fan
Toaster
Shower bucket/Shower shoes
Desk lamp
Comforter/Pillows
VCR/DVD player
Coffeemaker
Toiletries
Iron
Umbrella
Radio/Headphones
Hair dryer

There probably was more, but she couldn't think of
anything else. Her budget was four hundred dollars. She

hoped that was enough. Once she landed in Georgia she'd find a dollar store to purchase what she could. The rest she'd get at Target. Did they have Targets in Georgia? She sure hoped so.

She couldn't believe it. Two more days at home. That's all that was left. Then she'd be leaving Honey and Earl behind. Never to return, probably. After college she'd get her own place, hopefully room with Kenya for a few years. Then she'd get married. Get a house. A nice ranch-style with fences around the property that made you think they had horses. A Volvo in the circular drive.

Lark had it all figured out.

What was it they said about the best-laid plans, though?

There was a soft tap at the door.

"Come in."

The door slid open. Honey.

"Unless you've come to tell me I'm adopted and Oprah's my biological mom, and she wants me back, I don't want to hear it." Lark looked at her mother and smiled. "I've had enough heart-to-heart with you for one week, Mama."

"You've got a fresh mouth."

"Came by it naturally."

Honey was by her side. "What's that?"

Lark tapped the notepad with her pen. "List of some things I'm gonna need for school."

"Funny you should say that. I was coming to see about us going shopping."

Lark frowned. "I'll get it down there. I can't carry this stuff on a plane."

"That's true."

"Speaking of which. Daddy handled my flight reservations?"

"He did."

"What time I'm flying out?"

"You aren't."

"Excuse me?"

"My return flight from Georgia is five-fifteen, I believe," Honey said.

"Your return flight?"

Honey smiled. "Yes. We rented a car. I'm driving you. Leaving the car there. They can do that, you know. And then I'm flying back."

Lark's mouth dropped open into an O. She couldn't respond.

Honey picked up the notepad. "Let's see what's on this list. We've only got one day...."

chapter 23

Kenya

"TOld you Tommie and Blue were gonna end up together, Kenya."

"Happily ever after," I say.

Terrence closes the Eric Jerome Dickey novel, places it back on the table next to my bed. Over the course of three days he's read the 269-page paperback to me, cover to cover. It can get lonely in the hospital, even with Mama, Hollywood, Eric and Lark visiting me regularly throughout the days.

Terrence clasps his hands together, rises from a chair, stretches, yawns. "*Naughty or Nice*. Dickey did a good job with that one."

"He always does."

Terrence smiles.

Lark asked me if he was as cute as his namesake on *106 & Park*. I said cuter. I meant it, too. My Terrence has his salt-and-pepper cropped short. He wears glasses, sports a bushy mustache and smells like aftershave.

"How long you been married again?" I ask.

"Twenty-seven years this past June." He looks around, moves over to the footboard of my bed, knocks on it.

"Would've knocked on your table," he says when he sees me looking, "but that ain't wood. They don't make anything out of wood anymore."

"Superstitious, are we?"

"When it comes to marriage, you need a cross pendant, rabbit's foot, horseshoes, four-leaf clovers, *Claudine* on DVD..."

"*Claudine?*" I ask.

He sniffs his nose. "Diahann Carroll, Miss Kenya. A nice little dose of fantasy is good for every marriage."

"I have to get *Brown Sugar* then. A two-for-one."

Taye and Boris.

Mmm.

"You a long way off from marriage, Kenya," Terrence says. "Gotta get your degree first. Settle yourself in a career."

"True dat." But love is on my mind. "Any other advice?"

"Trust," he says, "which comes from honesty. Have to be friends, too. It's helpful if you and your husband actually enjoy being around each other. And most importantly, you need some of what I call that Rudyard Kipling."

"Rudyard Kipling?"

Terrence nods. "If you can fill the unforgiving minute/ with sixty seconds worth of distance run/ yours is the Earth and everything that's in it/ and—which is more—you'll be a man, my son." He pauses. "Or daughter."

"I've heard that before," I say.

"Poem is named 'If.' Stick-to-it-iveness, Kenya. That's the most important thing in a relationship."

"Never give up," I whisper.

"Ever," Terrence says.

"Could you do something for me?" I ask Terrence.

"Long as you don't ask me to read you *War and Peace.*"

"What?"

He waves me off. "What you need, Kenya?"

"Need you to dial a couple numbers for me, hold the phone. I have a few calls I need to make."

* * *

This time I don't fall asleep. I have on a touch of lipstick, a dash of perfume. My hair is neat, pulled back in a tight ponytail. All the clutter is cleared off my table. There's one bouquet of flowers left in the room—yellow tulips from Hollywood. Yes, Mama's Hollywood.

I smile as Donnell walks in the room.

It's funny. Watching Donnell slowly ease into my room, all kinds of images run through my head. Us walking through the park holding hands. Playing virtual reality games over at Dave & Buster's in Philadelphia.

Dancing in his parents' basement at one of his parties. Kissing in the dark of the movie theater.

"You wanted to see me?" Donnell asks.

"Yeah. I did."

"Wassup, Kenya? I'm here."

"Why don't you sit?"

He looks around. For a chair, I guess.

"Sit on the bed," I say.

"I'm okay standing."

"Please?"

He frowns. "I don't want to hurt you."

"I'm not made of glass, Donnell. Sit on the bed."

He sighs, but slides the table next to my bed out of the way, drops the side rail, eases onto the bed. "Okay. Wassup, Kenya?"

"How've you been?"

"Fine. Wassup?"

"You in a rush?"

"Kinda."

"Got a date?" I ask sweetly.

"Don't do that, Kenya."

I nod. He's right. "Do you hate me?" I ask.

"Why would I hate you?"

"I disturbed a pretty good thing."

"You did. That a cause for hate, though?"

His honesty is refreshing.

Terrence would give that a thumbs-up.

What did Terrence say?

Honesty, friendship, Rudyard Kipling.

"When you were standing on line to get my book signed, what were you thinking?" I ask.

"I hoped I didn't have to use the bathroom."

I giggle. "What else?"

"You'd be surprised, and happy."

"What made you buy me the Chrisette Michele CD?"

"You wanted it."

"The dolphin key chain?"

"You wanted it."

"The yogurt bars?"

"You love those."

"You've been a good friend," I say.

"I've tried my best, Kenya." He takes a deep breath. "Most of the time."

"Even before we were going out."

Donnell warned me about my ex. Ricky. He didn't want to see me get hurt. He picked me up when I did.

"Yes," Donnell says. "Even before we were going together."

"Hand me that cup of ice chips," I say. "My mouth is dry."

Donnell gets the cup, puts it to my lips. I open my mouth, tilt my head back. I crunch on a mouthful of ice shavings. My tongue dislodges itself from the roof of my mouth. Much better.

"More?" Donnell asks.

"I'm good."

He puts the cup back on the table.

"There was a party down in Georgia, at school. One of the sororities. The Deltas."

I smile at the memory.

Not the party per se.

Carolina. Tammy.

My sistergirlfriends.

"Okay," Donnell says.

"I ended up having to sing."

"Sorry I missed that. You have a beautiful voice. I never get tired of hearing you sing."

"After the party, this guy came up to me, complimented me. Chatted me up some. I ain't gonna lie…he was fly. Six-four. Ran track, so his body was right."

Donnell's jaw muscles tense.

He smiles.

But his eyes don't match the smile.

"He made a heavy play for me."

"JaMarcus," Donnell says.

I nod. "Yup."

"Okay."

"I was feeling him. I won't lie to you."

Donnell swallows.

"I understand what you said about Melyssa," I say. "How sometimes things just happen. It's crazy, but true."

Donnell closes his eyes and sighs long and hard.

"But nothing happened like that between me and JaMarcus," I say.

Donnell's eyes open. He searches me for the truth.

"Nothing," I repeat.

"Okay."

"You ever heard the poem 'If.' By Rudyard Kipling?"

"Yeah. Think so."

I repeat the line Terrence recited to me.

"Yeah," Donnell says.

"Stick-to-it-iveness."

"What's that?'

"I've got that," I say. "We've got that."

"Okay."

"I'm gonna need you to help me with my papers."

"What?"

"I still can't hold any heavy books, so I'm gonna need you to spot for me."

"What are you talking about, Kenya?"

"I could use a computer, but in the meantime we'll have to share your laptop."

"Kenya, slow down. You've lost me."

"Almost," I say. "But I smarted up."

"What?"

"Terrence made some calls for me. Well, he dialed. I spoke."

"Who is Terrence? What calls?"

Terrence dialed Donnell's number, of course.

And a few others.

I'd thought of several after Terrence agreed to make a couple calls for me. Lark. Had to call my homegirl. Mama. Had to let her know what was happening. A few others.

"Kenya?"

"I'll explain some other time," I say.

"I don't understand anything you've told me."

"It doesn't matter at the moment."

"Easy for you to say."

"I'm not going to school in Georgia, Donnell."

He frowns. "You haven't...? You're gonna be okay, aren't you?"

I smile. "Has nothing to do with my accident."

The frown is still on his face. "You're giving up on college."

"Oh, no. Never that."

I say *never that* the way I spell it in text messages.

Neva dat.

Donnell shakes his head. "I. Am. Lost."

I reach forward, take his hand in mine.

I don't mention Melyssa Bryan, or her visit, but she looms large in the room.

"We're going to school together," I say.

"What?"

"I'm staying in Jersey. Going to Rutgers with you."

His eyes widen, mouth falls open.

"Close your mouth, Donnell."

He does.

"Say something, Donnell."

"I...I don't know what to say, Kenya."

I loved when he called me YaYa.

It was cute.

But I'm Kenya.

And Donnell loves himself some Kenya.

What more could I ask for?

"Don't say anything." I squeeze his hand. "Kiss your girlfriend."

All we've been through the past few weeks, all the turmoil, confusion, pain and suffering, all of it disappears with Donnell's smile. He shakes his head, snickers, then leans forward.

And kisses his girlfriend.

chapter 24

Fiasco

"**TWO** spiderwebs."

Fiasco didn't reply. He chewed on a drink straw, stewed inside, felt a dangerous anger bubbling up just below the surface. He hadn't felt that way since just before he went to prison.

"Good thing no one was back there. That would've been a bad ending."

Fiasco ground his teeth, balled his hands in fists, kicked the dirt below his feet. A cloud of dirt rose up from the ground.

"World's Greatest MC? What does that mean? This big ol' bus. You some kind of entertainer?"

Fiasco eyed his travel bus. Two spiderwebs, bullet-hole punctures that cracked the two back windows on the right side of the bus. The back windows. Windows to the sleeping compartment.

"Need some cooperation from you, son."

Fiasco finally looked at the trooper. Cowboy hat over a crew cut. Weather-beaten tan, square jaw.

"We had just pulled up at the club," Fiasco said. "Yes, I'm an entertainer. I was scheduled to perform. The driver was parking, getting us settled. I heard shots. I ducked down. Didn't catch anything."

"Someone mentioned there being a caravan of Expeditions with tinted windows circling the lot right before the shooting. They drove off right after the shots were fired. But no one can say for sure the shots came from those vehicles. You see such a thing?"

"I ducked down," Fiasco repeated. "I didn't see anything."

"Just your dumb luck got your bus all shot up?"

Fiasco nodded. "Guess so."

Trooper Cowboy shook his head. "Some people have all the luck."

chapter 25

Kenya

It's hard to say goodbye. Better to just say see you soon. That's exactly what I tell Lark, my best friend.

"You're sure about this, Ken?" she says.

I nod, smile. "I've never been surer about anything."

She's sitting in the bed with me.

"The mighty twosome becomes a onesome."

"Onesome?"

"This is my moment. Don't intrude."

I laugh.

She does, too.

"The benefit concert should benefit someone other than me."

"School costs a grip. I'll take the money," Lark says.

More laughs.

"So your mom is driving you?"

Lark smirks. "Yup," she says. "Honey's ushering her daughter into adulthood."

"Adulthood, huh?"

"My clock is ticking, Ken."

"I'm happy for you."

Lark takes my hand, squeezes it. A friend's gesture—same kind of thing Donnell does. "I'm happy for the both of us," she says.

I bite my lip, nod, but keep silent.

"You're gonna be okay, Ken?" she says.

"I am...but look. We need to establish some parameters for our relationship if we're gonna make it work."

Lark snickers. "I agree."

"At least ten text messages every day."

"And two live calls," Lark adds.

"As opposed to a dead one."

She wrinkles her nose. "Smart-ass."

"We have to make it a point to see one another as regularly as possible. I suggest we get together every six weeks or so, when you come to see Donovan."

"And you have to get your future husband to drive you down some, too, Ken."

I nod. "Will do."

"I'm going to be off in a strange and dangerous land by myself, so feel free to send gifts, care packages."

"You ain't going to Baghdad, Lark."

"Without you there...it's gonna feel like it."

And we cry.

chapter 26

Eric

I'd called Fiasco more than twenty times.

He didn't pick up once.

They'd been reporting on the shooting of his tour bus all day on Hot 97. Angie Martinez was fearful the rivalry between Fiasco and Yung Chit would end with someone dead. Hearing her say that word, dead, really put everything into perspective.

Fiasco was my friend.

He'd picked me up when I was at my lowest.

I'd been posting negative comments about Yung Chit on my MySpace page. And people had been reading. My last post had garnered over sixty comments—most of 'em hating on me for hating on Yung Chit. He was the darling of the moment, hip-hop's reigning king. I could see that from my own little world perspective. I couldn't imagine what Fiasco was dealing with.

I'd been trying to throw Fiasco some support by tearing down Yung Chit. But all I'd really done was add fuel to the fire. If Fiasco ended up hurt, I was partly responsible. I dialed his number yet again.

Straight to voice mail like my last few calls.

Dayum!

chapter 27

Fiasco

They were calling the concert at Kenya's school a Dirty South production.

Fiasco shook his head, laughed to himself. Where did it all go wrong? All he wanted to do was make good music, leave a legacy. What was his legacy gonna be now? The last man standing in the feud with Yung Chit or the first man down? Either way, the music would take a backseat.

The cruelest part of the whole thing was that the beef had pushed Yung Chit's album sales over three million. Fiasco hadn't even picked up enough new sales to reach the elusive gold status—500,000 records. He couldn't even sell that anymore. Couldn't even sell that after trading jabs with the hottest rapper in the game, after getting the kind of media exposure in the past few weeks he hadn't seen in years. Fiasco's face was all over the Internet. Talk of his beef with Yung Chit dominated the airwaves, both television and radio. Rap lovers were getting a constant diet of Fiasco. And they were pushing away from the table without even taking a bite. He was finished in the game.

What did it matter?

What did anything matter?

He looked out the window of the bus. Toya was back in South Carolina at the Hilton. Mya wasn't around anymore. He'd cut his entourage down considerably, and those that remained weren't really friends. They hung around, kept him from getting too lonely, but they played no significant role in his life.

Only one thing to do.

Hit that stage and let the chips fall where they may.

"How much longer 'fore we get to the college?" he called out to his driver.

"An hour, maybe a li'l less."

Fiasco fell back into his seat.

In three hours he'd walk out on that stage, in Yung Chit country, and give the crowd his middle finger.

They could hit him with whatever they had.

He'd take it.

chapter 28

Eric

I noticed plenty of security. There was a wall of incredibly huge men with peacemakers on their belts, and Kevlar vests covering their torsos, guarding the perimeter of the stage. The concert was taking place outside. The Georgia air was nice, smelled fresher than the air in Jersey, for sure. There must've been eight thousand or so in the crowd. I'd heard more than one person mumble they were coming to see Fiasco's execution. It was definitely a Yung Chit crowd.

Yung Chit was on record saying he had gunners everywhere.

Despite all the security by the stage, I'd walked over to the auditorium and come through the gates unchecked. The school definitely wasn't making it very difficult for Yung Chit's gunners. That worried me sick. My stomach was a bundle of nerves. This was a fight that Fiasco couldn't engage in alone. So I was here.

I'd texted Lark, asked her to step to the back of the auditorium, by the concession stands. She walked up, her eyes squinted, lines in her forehead. "Eric?" She had a glow to her skin. College was working for her, even if she was only a day into her higher-education pursuit. "Kenya?" she asked.

The worry was heavy in her voice. I suppose my appearance would have worried me too if the shoe were on the other foot.

"Kenya's fine," I said.

"What are you doing here?"

"Came to support Fiasco." I said *support,* but I was thinking *save.*

Lark smiled wide, embraced me.

I hugged her back, of course, but we didn't have much time. Fiasco was hitting the stage in about ten minutes, from what I understood.

"I need to get back to see Fiasco," I said.

"You'd have to speak to Carolina on that. I didn't have anything to do with this."

"Can you get me to her?"

Lark frowned. "Don't even know where she is."

"Can you find out?"

She studied me briefly. "Let me see what I can do."

chapter 29

Fiasco

NORMALLY he prayed right before he went on stage. Not that he was all that close to God, but it was something he did regularly. It set him at ease, relaxed his mind. Your mind had to be relaxed when you stepped on a stage in front of a crowd. Too many performers had gotten in that position, forgotten words to songs or delivered them poorly because their voices cracked. He'd performed thousands of times, in small clubs and even large arenas. Even at Madison Square Garden that one time, which seemed like a million years ago but was only four. No matter how many times he performed, though, it never really got any easier. It took nerves of steel to get up in front of people, make them enjoy your music, make them bob their heads to your songs. So he usually prayed for comfort, for strength. Usually.

Today he wasn't.

He'd heard the talk. Yung Chit and his gunners.

His bus was evidence that Yung Chit wasn't just talking.

He thought of the two spiderwebs right in the windows of the compartment where he laid his head at night. That was a violation of the highest order.

Now I lay me down to sleep, I pray to the Lord my soul to keep
If I should die...
Nope. He wouldn't pray.
It was what it was.

chapter 30

Eric

"**come**, Eric."

I sighed a breath of relief, followed Lark. We went back out through the gates, crossed over behind the large bleachers of the auditorium and came up on a grouping of buildings. "Fiasco's in there," she said. "They have Yung Chit on the other side of the field."

I nodded.

"Security's no joke. You're worried about your boy?"

"Yes."

She searched my eyes. "Someone just told me Fiasco's bus got shot up? That true?"

"He hasn't answered my calls."

She gripped my hands, squeezed. "I love you, Poseys. Please be careful."

"Ditto," I said.

Then I took another deep breath and headed in to see Fiasco.

He was standing in front of the mirror, throwing punches at his reflection.

I stepped in, closed the door behind me. "Syke Tyson," I said.

He turned slowly, eyed me. "E."

There wasn't much life in his voice. He didn't appear surprised.

"I came to ask you not to go on stage," I said.

He shook his head. So he did have some life. "Can't do that, son. You know that."

"Your bus got shot at?"

"Two spiderwebs," he said.

"What?"

"Yeah," he said. "My bus got shot at."

"Don't go on that stage."

"There ain't anything you can say to keep me off that stage, E."

I nodded. He was probably right. I'd considered that before I came.

I pivoted around, moved back to the door and turned the knob.

I stuck my head out into the hall, made a motion with my hand.

I moved aside so she could enter the room, then closed the door behind her. I stepped to a corner of the room, made myself comfortable in the shadows.

Fiasco stopped cold. "Mya?"

"Ruben."

I hunched my eyes in surprise. *Ruben?*

"What are you doing here?"

She shrugged. "I came to see my brother."

"You shouldn't be here."

"That makes two of us."

Fiasco frowned. "I have to do this performance."

"And possibly get yourself killed. Why?"

"I'll be fine, Mya."

"Tell that to Afeni Shakur, or Voletta Wallace."

Those were the mothers of Tupac and Biggie.

Fiasco sighed. "Album tanked. This is all I know, Mya."

"So make another album. Nobody handed any of this to you. You hustled, grinded. Keep grinding, Ruben."

"Been tough without you around. You were always the voice of wisdom. I've made some bad decisions."

She moved closer to him. "Me, too," she said.

"I need you back in the fold."

"You'll stay off that stage?"

"The college is expecting me to—"

Mya cut him off. "Eric has a plan. It's a damn good one, too."

"Yeah?"

She told him my plan.

Fiasco looked over at me. I nodded.

He made a fist, pounded it against his chest, against his heart.

I swallowed, looked at the time stamp on my cell phone. "It's showtime," I said.

A week later there'd be footage getting a lot of love on YouTube.

A scrawny, reformed nerd from the Dirty Jersey would commandeer the stage at a concert in Georgia. He'd come out, to the surprise of the crowd that was expecting the rapper Fiasco, and he'd rap the lyrics from a Fiasco song. Then he'd rap the lyrics from a Yung Chit song. Then he'd rap the lyrics to one final song.

Queen Latifah.

"U.N.I.T.Y."

By the end of the third song, it would be pandemonium.

A chant would rise to the sky.

Yung Chit, Yung Chit, Yung Chit.

And then a second chant.

Fiasco, Fiasco, Fiasco.

Both rappers would come out and end their beef, right there.

They'd embrace on stage, give one another a pound.

There'd even be talk of doing an album together.

That scrawny, reformed nerd from New Jersey would even get to spit a hot sixteen on that album.

Who knew he had skills, too?

PEACE YO WE OUT!